Joy Falls

Barbara Allen

Crooked Hearts Press

*You shall love your crooked neighbor
with your crooked heart.*

— W. H. Auden

Joy Falls

Published by Crooked Hearts Press
Tucson, Arizona

ISBN: 978-0-578-27485-0 (paperback)
ISBN: 978-0-578-27486-7 (ebook)
LCCN: 2022919459

Cover art by Cathy Larson
Cover design by Lori Conser

Other books published by Crooked Hearts Press:

Eleanor Wilner, *Gone to Earth* (2021)

Janice Dewey, *How to Feed a Horse* (2021)

For James Dean Allen, Jr.
and William Cronin

Acknowledgments

There is no book without Janice L. Dewey and Crooked Hearts Press. Thank you.

Several people have carefully read this manuscript—so much so that I have worried about their sanity: Kathleen Allen, Deb Jane, Barbara Restin, Mary Cooney, and the aforementioned Janice; thank you for your kindness, honesty, commitment to this book especially when I didn't have it myself. Bob Richards made sure I had physical space for writing and calmed me when I was sure technology was trying to eat my manuscript. Mirto provided all sorts of space, thank you.

Part of this book was published in *The American*.

The journey has always included Bill, Betsy, Dean, Nancy, Kathy, Peter, Ellen, Patty, Michael and their partners and children, especially Alana. Vicki, Lis, and soulmate, Sheila, thank you.

Especially, especially, especially: W. C. E.

Frank learns to drive

It took me seven years to find the right teacher. I admit it: I am cheap, so I determined my first and best option was a family member. I tried my wife, but she used the wrong tone (panicked). My brother-in-law was too much like Mr. Rogers. I approached my twelve-year-old nephew. I figured if someone that young smoked, as my nephew did, he probably also knew how to drive a car. I was right, and things were going well until my wife caught on. She put a halt to it, said it was not appropriate. I feared sometimes for my wife; she could be so bourgeois. I mean, who says words like "appropriate" besides a member of the middle class or maybe a fourth-grade PE teacher?

My wife, Joy, was expecting our first child at the time and did not want to drive herself to the hospital when she went into labor. She said it would not be safe. She gave me an ultimatum—get a driver's license, even if I had to pay, or she would ask her sister to drive her and be with her during the delivery of the baby. I hate my sister-in-law.

I finally settled on a driving school called Bulldog Enterprises. The school's owner, Ralph Ensign, was African American, a discharged vet who had lost his right arm in combat. The bulldog of the school's name, I learned while talking to Ralph that first time, referred to his determination to learn to drive with one arm and his fight with the state to allow him to set up a driving school.

"It wasn't easy," he explained to me over the phone before we started our lessons. "I had to demonstrate to the state that I could be steady while driving. You can if you place your one hand on the top and center part of the steering wheel, always."

I asked, "Do you take students who have two hands?" Ralph said he did, and we scheduled our first meeting.

Our first lesson took place in the same church parking lot my nephew had taken me to. I had to admit I felt some relief in not having to inhale secondhand smoke while learning the difference between park, first, and second.

I was jazzed after my first lesson. Ralph and I had quite a bit in common. I sensed this; I did not actually talk with him about it. Ralph and I were marginalized. We both had challenges. Mine were class-related—this was my assessment of my difficulties; this was before my diagnosis. I will get to that later. As an example of the class strife my wife and I had, let me explain how we disagreed on where to eat hamburgers. She preferred to eat expensive hamburgers and to have them brought to her on a plate, Dijon mustard and homemade potato chips on the side.

I said, "Why not get the cheap ones you can get at the drive-in?" There was not much difference, and with free refills, it could be quite a good deal.

She didn't like the noise or the saltiness. Her attitude bothered me, except for the salt part, which I thought could be dealt with the next day by drinking plenty of water. I thought her love of expensive hamburgers was silly and played into the silly thought that expense equals value.

I like to look at what the middle class does and do the opposite. I was diagnosed with a manic-depressive disorder after a spending binge at the dollar store, admittedly not the first time. This is why Joy, I later learned, had the owner call her every time I went there. It was her decision to take me to the doctor. We received the diagnosis the same day Joy's pregnancy test came back positive. My diagnosis, I thought, gave Ralph, my driving instructor, and me even more in common. His physical disability and his veteran status and his skin color. Traditional life for both of us, I assumed, was challenging.

The reason I'd never gotten my driver's license prior to this was my fear of other people's lack of, well, intelligence. I understood the rules of the road, but did they? Fundamentally, I did not want to share anything like laws or restaurants with my fellow citizens. Joy accepted and forgave this attitude of superiority, though she did on occasion call it bullshit—fearful and arrogant. She could get going when she got angry. If she wasn't terribly angry, she redefined my behavior as "hostile shyness."

She loved making things layered and complex. In her world, I was an undiscovered planet of nuance and texture. I thought she was full of it, not rational but a rationalizer. I knew who I was more than she knew who she was. I have been called arrogant, I know. My world was different from the one Joy was familiar with. Raised by drunks and the underclass, I had to invent myself. I had to hide and pursue my love of ideas and culture. Joy, like many in the middle class, had those handed to her. I am arrogant, but I earned my arrogance. I am also scared as shit, I admit.

Joy, I thought, could probably handle my diagnosis. Frankly, she'd had a long list of disappointments and shocks. She had a mother who hated her, and her favorite friend died at age eighteen. Not just died, was murdered. In my case, she got so she could tell when I was going over the edge. For instance, when I was decorating the front yard with used bike parts, she took me to the doctor. I alternated between resentment toward and appreciation of her. In more lucid moments, I understood she suffered my mania with worry and fear, especially for the children. Other times, I felt so punished by her with her plans to get me well. Eventually, she finessed it so I was always supervised when I was with the children. This was after my final breakdown.

Through the years, I knew how I could be unrecognizable to her and to myself. That was hard. Hard for both of us. It was beyond being disembodied. If you are disembodied, you can watch yourself, but I could not. Something else had completely moved in and taken over. I was not recognizable to myself. At some point, I started being hospitalized—my idea to be placed in psychiatric units, not Joy's. Except, once, she did have me placed in the state psychiatric unit. What a hellhole. No light. No smart doctors. Bedraggled staff. No one deserved that. What a betrayal!

My cooking habits were another barometer Joy used to measure my instability, though that was a bit more challenging, she admitted in those moments when we could be lighthearted. She loved my cooking. I introduced her to Thai eggplant and taught her how to use a peeler to get at the heart of cumin or garlic. When the curry became too hot or too many dishes were used—seven pots when the meal required only two—the doctor was called.

Her self-assignment to monitor my mental health made her cranky, especially while she was pregnant and my diagnosis was new. Eventually, scrutinizing my behavior for the signs of my instability became second nature to her. I was aware that she was aware of my "signs." It got so I was no longer sensitive about this psychological cat-and-mouse game. It was just the way it was. Joy and I had a long conversation, and I finally agreed that it would be OK to send the doctor a note asking about the possibility of our child having my mental-health challenges.

"Oh, why not put off worrying about it for now?" the doctor advised. We tried, even as it remained a shadow that was not large but rested softly between us.

After three driving lessons, Ralph called my wife. I learned this many years later. "Listen, I really need the money, but if your husband doesn't quit talking during these lessons, he's going to fail his driver's test, and I have a hundred percent success rate. I'm thinking of dropping him."

I guess Joy cried. After what must have been a great deal of negotiation with Ralph, Joy joined the two of us on the driving lessons. She lay down on the backseat with a black silk shade over her eyes because she and Ralph had both agreed that she should not watch. It wouldn't help her, and it wouldn't help me. Her large pregnant belly was a nice arch I could see in the rearview mirror. And her presence did quiet me down.

"River Road," Ralph said, "is the best place to learn to be

steady. Frank, place your hands on the wheel at the ten and two positions and have your eyes guide you, not your hands, through any curvy road like River."

Joy knew that I was nervous, I am sure, and could feel the car get jerky. After several tense moments, Ralph told me to pull the car over and said sternly, "Relax. Own the road. Focus on the road just a few feet ahead of you." After several false starts, Joy suggested, with her blindfold on, that we pull over. She said, "Frank, get out of the car."

She took my hands in hers and practiced the Lamaze breathing we had been reading about in the evenings. Her blindfold was now resting on her forehead. Her strategy worked. I relaxed, and with a few exceptions, I began to hug the curve. Fairly or unfairly, I don't know, I usually dismissed Joy's ideas. Her strength is not her rationality. Her persistence is her strength. Doing Lamaze breathing may have been a good idea, and it may have been a bad one. In Joy's hands, it was inevitable—breathing and hugging the road, I did them both.

Joy fully expected my discontent with my fellow humans to change once the baby was born. I mean, she had changed, she argued. She did not like children, but after holding her newborn niece, she changed her mind. There was nothing more beautiful than the smell of a newborn's skin and nothing so well earned as the red splotches on her niece's scalp because of her arduous passage through the birth canal, Joy insisted. We read Walt Whitman on the night the baby was conceived, "The Wound-Dresser." I know that Walt, as Joy and I called him, is famous for "Song of Myself" and roaming and being at one with men, women and children, etc.

But "The Wound Dresser" is inexplicably heartfelt for this egocentric guy, gorgeously generous to the wounded and the horror they have experienced on our behalf.

Eventually, I received my license. To celebrate, I bought two cases of mangoes at the farmers' market. Joy had never had mangoes before she was pregnant. She ate them all in one sitting. I took pictures. I had never seen such a thing. Joy was quite large at this point and sucked on the large seeds very thoroughly. We made jokes, etc.

We still owned just one car, and out of habit, Joy was the default driver. The Saturday before our son, Jake, was born, she dropped me off at the grocery store for sale items. She went to the grocery store across the street for other store items. When she was done, she drove to the grocery store where I was shopping, but I had left to meet her at the grocery store where she was shopping. This was a common problem for us: forgetting to check in regarding life's essential details, where you will be and when.

We finally caught up with each other after crossing paths for nearly an hour. It was I who found Joy. She was in the car crying. "What's the matter?" I demanded.

Joy said, in between gulps, "I began to wonder what it would be like if you were dead. I wondered what life would be like without you." She was laughing and crying. "I would need to learn to cook. No one would ever find me beautiful again. I would miss your voice," and finally, "You're OK?" She was half-demanding and half-scared.

"Yeah, and I found a deal on mangoes."

"Oh," she said, "how good was the deal on mangoes?" I told her.

Jake was born a week later. Followed two years later by Tess, and three years after that there was Mia. I think it was a good run. I am a manic-depressive, and I learned to drive.

Joy helps Frank, who has been in a car accident and is also very depressed

Frank and I had three children: Jake, Tess and Mia. In the semi-good days, Frank was a semi-good father. He was good at incorporating the children into his own tasks: cooking, washing, and shopping.

However, he did not observe the children's universe: he did not get on his knees and see from their angle. It was I who felt compelled to play trains or have tea parties. I was not by nature interested in these activities, but in the name of maternal generosity, I spent endless amounts of time playing games I thought a little boring, even if they were created from the beautiful heads of my imaginative children. If I asked Frank to pinch-hit for me, he was agreeable but was likely to reorder the child-centered activities. He would place the infant or toddler seat on the washing machine while he loaded the dryer. He played with tiny feet and read at the same time. His multitasking approach, I admit, infuriated me.

But things got bad, very bad. More and more, Frank's depression was the norm. He would have bouts of mania.

In the beginning, his soirees into exuberance had a family component: lookalike denim jean jackets for everyone or rubber sandals for all or Chairman Mao hats for the girls. Over the years, both the depression and the mania became more curious—three hundred pads of paper with a logo from the Winnebago dealership, pinball-machine parts— and he needed more and more validation that the boxes and boxes of stuff were a good idea. I lost the energy for the fiction. Whether or not Frank's depression was fed by my inability to go along with his schemes often kept me up at night. Inevitably, he would surrender to the bed, sometimes at his house, sometimes at mine. He could sleep anywhere and anytime.

Sometimes, even though Frank had moved out, I needed his assistance. On the one hand, I hoped he would appreciate being needed. On the other hand, I did not want to tax him. One bright winter morning, the routine at the household was disrupted. The teenagers, Jake and Tess, needed a ride to school because the bus drivers were on strike, and that disrupted the morning routine. Normally, I drove Mia to her middle school, which was on the other side of town, and the older children took the school bus.

I asked Frank to take Mia to school, even knowing he had morning routines and he was not fond of disruptions. Besides, he was in a depressive mode, more fearful than usual. I knew the request would not be welcome, and I was relieved when Frank agreed to it.

Maybe Mia would be adorable; maybe she would speak her youthful wisdom and say, "War sucks and is really bad for the economy too. We should say no to blood and money." Then Frank could feel parental pleasure and be pleased.

I drove the teenagers, Jake and Tess, and tried to remember not to talk to them. It annoyed them so early in the morning. Instead, I found myself wistful. My children were preparing to slip away, move on from me. To get their independence, my older children had turned on me.

I waited for the stoplight to turn colors. With bittersweetness and my fist on my cheek, I thought of the tedious hours playing games and inventing ways for them to feel safe. Now I was the dangerous stranger I warned them against. The person who asked the inappropriate questions. I knew it was inevitable, but still I was surprised at their vehemence. In their drive to be without me, they were no longer able to understand how much I loved them. How I'd always loved them. How I knew they deserved so much more than me.

I thought about my last fight with Jake—just last night. He accused me of trying to cure him of his dyslexia with neurologists, phonetics teachers, hippie tutors who had him making the letters out of clay. Why couldn't I just let him be? Tess had her own list of grievances—I'd had the nerve to marry someone with a genetic proclivity toward mental illness. Because of me, Tess had inherited the genes for a less-than-attractive nose. Tess's grievances were delivered in a seething whisper, more sullen than Jake's.

When I arrived at the high school, Jake jumped out of the car and slammed the door with his foot while completing the buttoning of his shirt. I couldn't help but admire his fluidity.

Why wasn't my patchwork approach to family working? We were together, weren't we? In a way? But everyone was isolated. At night, my house was like a film I had once seen. It was set in a hotel room, with each of the guests slamming the door behind them to be sullen or miserable in their own way. The camera, though, lingered on the empty hallway. My life was like that more often than I liked, my choices seeming to be sullenness or emptiness.

Fifteen minutes after arriving at work, I got the call. It was Frank. After dropping Mia off, there had been an accident, Mountain and Seneca. He was OK, but could I come right away to help him? Of course I could. I left, shouting to the secretary, the lovely assistant who always shook her head at my escapades, the reasons for my departure. I drove up Mountain toward Seneca, and about three blocks before the accident, I saw random clothes, scattered pots and pans, ties, corn oil in a large plastic container. I realized I had not been paying close attention to Frank. At some point, without my noticing, his mania had slipped into his car and got stuck there when his pendulum went back to depression. I saw, too, that the car was being held together with duct tape and bungee cords. When did that happen? How did I fail to notice?

Amazingly, the accident was not Frank's fault. A kind woman on her way to volunteer at the hospital had hit him on the passenger side, spinning the car around, undoing the duct tape, causing the contents to tumble out. Frank's innocence did not stop the police officer from telling me that Frank was the weirdest dude he had ever seen. The officer suggested Frank might need a breathalyzer exam as he had failed a field sobriety test. I asked, "What's a field sobriety test?"

The officer explained, "Well, I have observed that he cannot make eye contact, and his physical motions are slow."

That made me laugh. It was fun to laugh. "Well, that is just his universe," I said.

The officer did not see anything to laugh about. I promised I would be responsible for Frank for the rest of the day.

Frank was lying on the dirt next to the car , which must have contributed to the officer's perception that Frank was inebriated. I admonished him to get up. He sat up but stayed on the ground. "This has disrupted my fragile personality, but I do not blame you, Joy." He was too distraught to pick up the many things that had spilled from the car, and could I pick up the contents, he asked. Of course I could.

I walked three blocks to the south, picking up about fifteen cotton shirts in my arms. I made three other trips, picking the items up according to categories: bathroom, kitchen, miscellaneous (empty car-oil containers, a *Life* magazine from 1967, notebooks). "Can I throw any of these away?"

"No," Frank replied, "but can you put them in your car? I am too devastated to deal with them right now. Some of those shirts are all cotton and Ralph Lauren. I got them at the thrift store's Two-for-Wednesday sale."

"They can be in my car for two days only," I said.

I called work to say I would be gone for the day and drove Frank to his home, put him to bed, grabbed his laptop and went to wait at the scene of the accident for a tow truck to come. I had a vague memory that Seneca, the Roman philosopher, was a great believer in the inevitability of longing and even grief. I knew I would have a long wait for the car to be towed, and I took the laptop to investigate.

Seneca, I learned, was a tutor to Emperor Nero

before Caligula sent him into exile. I had remembered my humanities class almost correctly. Seneca advocated the importance of fate: how the best we can do is be stoic, and with that comes a certain dignity. "Mr. Seneca," I said out loud, "I agree. I will be stoic in spite of this shit!"

Seneca was forced to kill himself. He betrayed the emperor. I could not determine if the betrayal was personal or political and supposed it did not really matter. Obviously, nothing would be worked out between the emperor and Seneca. In the Roman tradition, he cut his wrists while taking a warm bath.

Because this method of suicide is slow, family and friends came in to say goodbye.

The tow truck took quite a while to come. Two hours. After reading about Seneca and Caligula, I thought I would look up the names of ancient female philosophers. But I did not know the names of any. Only the poet Sappho, so I typed in the name. What I discovered was a term paper written by Rita Carlson, a third-grader from Philadelphia, who had won the state essay contest. Her subject was Sappho. The essay said, in part, that "Sappho's time was a time of change. Colonies along the Mediterranean coast flourished; tyranny and democracy were competing. This was the world Sappho lived in, though she appears to have written mostly about love."

I wondered about Rita. How was her hair prepared for the award ceremony? If it was blond, did she put fresh flowers in it? If dark hair, then a yellow band. Because I thought Sappho would recommend that in her ancient wisdom. I hoped the award ceremony was a good occasion for the whole family and to celebrate they went to the pancake house on a Sunday. I hoped Rita's parents were happy and made love in the afternoon after the award ceremony—with the curtains open and the sunlight coming in.

That they napped and used Rita's headband to tie their hands together, prayerlike.

I fell asleep in the driver's seat waiting for the tow truck. It was a heavy sleep, and the tow-truck driver startled me. In my confusion, I admit I was overly polite, trying to explain the junk in Frank's car. I said it was not mine. But then I realized this explanation might make me suspect—if it wasn't mine, why was I sitting here seemingly protecting the sundry junk?

"What is this stuff to you?" the driver asked. I had indeed raised suspicions. At first, because I was still partly in a dream, I considered telling the tow-truck driver my and Frank's story. How we loved each other rather quickly after meeting and made marriage plans that I postponed because Mother was ill.

The tow-truck driver, like me, like everyone I knew, simply wanted to do his job. So I said, "I am doing a favor for my ex-husband. How much will this cost?" The issue of money reassured the driver. His shirt was inscribed with the name Sam. And he began to lower the back of the truck to lift the car onto the bed of the vehicle. Feeling useless, I went to the corner and pretended to be looking for something down the street—something other than a day with Frank's car, Seneca and a tow truck. Eventually, and with resignation, I turned around and paid Frank's towing bill.

Two weeks after the accident, the shirts and the broken bottles were still in my car. I had asked Frank about them, but he was not quite strong enough to deal with the contents yet. I waited another week and then drove to Frank's one-room casita. He had turned his carport into a reservoir for stuff he had collected: broken lamps, a bookcase with no shelves. He had taken the backseat out of the van and used it as a couch. Frank was not home, so I placed the shirts from the spill onto the "couch." I allowed myself to throw the other items in the dump. Two weeks later, I again went to Frank's house and asked him if he had noticed I dropped his shirts off for him. His phone had been disconnected. No, he did not notice that.

"Well," I said, wasting no time, "I need to go purchase some ribbons for Mia's hair."

"Why?" he asked.

"Just in case," I replied, "just in case there is a need for them, a ceremony or an award. Just something in her life might require them." Frank offered to try to find some at the thrift store; he was on his way there. "No, no," I responded, "I am looking for something in particular—something fresh or new."

This comment hurt Frank's feelings. While at the secondhand store, he must have purchased a spool of Christmas ribbon as a gift for Mia and me. A few days later, he came to my house. I was lying on my bed doing what I called the "despair lounge": ankles crossed, fingers on my chin, the room dark, except the curtain cracked a little for a sliver of light to spill in. Frank rang the bell twice and then turned around and walked away, leaving the ribbon on the doorstep. I eventually got up and saw it there. I threw it away.

Mia does not want to be the smartest girl in class anymore

My mother tries to be funny by being ludicrous. The other day, we were driving, and she says, "Oh, by the way, I forgot to tell you I've joined a cult, and we will be moving to Plaster City, Arizona, where it is 103 degrees during the day but only 102 at night."

I smile. Her comment is funny in a farfetched way. I also know her hope is that I will say to myself, "Things could be worse than they already are. In addition to having a mentally ill father and a druggy brother and a rather high-strung sister, I could also be living in a place called Plaster City." My mother is very tan, long-legged, tired-looking and distracted. She does not finish sentences.

I used to be more talkative. I even interrupted to the point that my aunt Debra had to have a private conversation with me about it. I had so much to say and really wanted to say it to adults.

Because I knew they were in charge. I wanted them to know I was not pleased about wars, and I believed in virtue or at least what I read in the book *Greek Myths for Chil-*

dren. Who was going to carry my message and deliver it to God? Not me. Maybe an adult would. Those were my type of thoughts when I was younger. I would think about these things quite a bit when I would lie on the couch and have my mother rub my feet.

When I got tired of worrying during these times, I would go ask my brother, Jake, to wrestle with me, and he would—before he took drugs and started to ignore me. Actually, it was worse than ignoring me. He would look at me as if I was familiar but he did not know me.

Looking at things from a distance, looking back at my five-year-old self, I was unfair to Tess, even though she was my older sister. I helped myself to her books, her dolls, and her nifty art supplies. I know she thought in exchange for my thievery she would get to treat me like a doll—meaning speaking to me slowly, loudly and using a baby voice. I hated this. It made me so grumpy, but I tried to remember that I should let her treat me this way because her behavior was an exchange for me taking her possessions. Still, I would find myself stomping away from her. No matter how many times this happened, she was startled and hurt that I still lost my patience and refused to let her treat me so childishly. I knew I was always breaking a silent agreement between us, and this compromised my secret desire to be her buddy. I wanted her to be my buddy because she was good at being able to pretend she was a grown-up. She would walk around with a pad in her hand and a broken phone to her ear and take notes and say, "Yup, yup, what is your timeline?" I thought it was very cool, and maybe she was going to share the note-taking with me.

Right now, as a girl of almost twelve, my own personal goal is to quit being the smartest person in class. My name is Mia, but I have a nickname: My-a-nerd. I admit it is funny and has a ring to it. This is not what annoys me. It is not being anonymous. I hate teachers smiling at me as if to suggest we are in the same club. Or my friends not just asking me questions about homework but also treating me as if I am a game-show contestant. I am tired of it.

I do not tell my mother any of these things—how I hate being noticed by my teachers and friends. I do not mind discussing ideas with my mom but only when it is my idea to start the conversation. While driving today, I brought up how you can be vulnerable and tough. Like in the movie *Juno*, where the teenager gets pregnant and is scared about this at the same time she is dealing with yucky adults. "I think that is a lot to handle," I said to my mother. "You know, early pregnancy, weird parents."

After I said this, my mom said, "Just for the record, if you get pregnant under the age of eighteen, I get to decide what happens, so don't get pregnant. In fact, don't ever get pregnant, I mean, unless you want to get pregnant. But you can't probably really want to until, let's say, hmmm, not until a very long time."

"Mom," I say, "I am an eleven-year-old girl, almost twelve. Do you really need to have a talk about birth control? I actually have more pressing issues."

"Oh, oh, I am sorry, honey." Then silence. Then, "Umm, you don't really want to talk about this stuff?" As she taps on the steering wheel.

"Mom, this is a car. It is not a counseling office, not an

espresso shop; put your coffee down." I hate to be harsh with her, but parents can be sort of like Pluto—a good argument can be made that it does not qualify for its planet status.

"Hmmm," says my mom, "back to *Juno* and being vulnerable. Do you feel vulnerable?" Can you believe it? Perhaps she is not teachable. But I just shut up. I can see it coming, and it finally does: "Your father and his mental illness. You know he still loves you." My signal to count to ten and try to calm myself down. Does she not know how I know she needs to turn every conversation into a way to talk about *it*?

My mom lost her job a while ago. That night we were sitting on the couch, kind of holding hands and just sitting. My father arrived suddenly and started to bang on windows. I think he was saying he understood the meaning of our names. Also, "The time for action is now," things like that. We were scared; my mom called her brother. Long story short, my father spent quite a bit of time in the hospital. According to my uncle, Michael, he is in a house now with lots of people like him.

I do not say anything, but Uncle Michael's statement is wrong. Others are not like my father. I read an email he sent my mom; I was rubbing her neck and read over her shoulders. The email from my father said his roommates were drug users and he had to eat corn dogs for dinner. I know he wanted my mother to feel bad. And she does. I can tell by a certain squint her eyes and mouth can do at the same time.

Another problem with Uncle Michael's statement: I can Google psychosis like anyone else, "break with reality." Psychotics each have their particular psychosis—my father cannot be with others like him; no others are like him. This does not mean I love him or I do not love him. As I told my mom's friend Angela because I was alone with her, "My dad is my dad, and so I love him. If I met him on the street, I would not choose him for a friend or a dad."

My mom makes sure she talks to two people each day, I have noticed. Her sister Debra and her friend Angela. She talks to her friend Roxanne only once a week. I guess because Roxanne doesn't live here. When she talks to Debra, each conversation starts with my mom saying something about Jake: "Today was a good day" or "Not sure what his plans are. You ask him if you need to know. I want to mind my own business." Minding her own business is a new concept for my mom, and I know she is trying to learn this because she started going to meetings a while ago for parents of recovering drug users like what my brother, Jake, is.

When she talks to Angela, each conversation starts very differently. Today she said to Angela, "When your parents moved here from New Jersey, how did they get here?" Then Angela tells her, and my mom laughs and asks more questions. Eventually, Angela is going to tell her something sensible to do.

The other day, Angela told her to see a professional bra fitter.

"Really," I heard my mom say. "A professional bra fitter? I didn't know that was a profession." If Angela thinks the assignment is very important, like a pedicure, she will pick my mom up to make sure the task happens.

Sometimes I get to spend the night by myself at Angela's. Even if Angela kind of ignores me, I am not bothered by that. In one of the rooms of their house, they have a pinball machine. Angela's husband, Tom, taught me to play. I am pretty good. It is also the place where I discovered the book

A Tree Grows in Brooklyn. I have read it several times and read it each time I am at their house. I don't love it because the girl has a weird but loving family like I do. I love it because Brooklyn seems far away, and the landscape, I imagine, is gritty and has a certain grayness even in summer. Where I live it can be extremely hot and bright, and everything outside seems exactly the same.

Except at Angela's house. She has four different patios. I am not kidding—north, south, east, west. At her house, I always have a different view, a different world, depending on where I am sitting. It makes me feel like a queen in heaven. Can you imagine different views, reading and a pinball machine? Angela has rules, and I don't mind obeying them even if I am a little embarrassed when I learn I am in violation: elbows off the table, absolutely no clothes on the floor. My favorite part is sometimes Angela just hugs me and says, "You are amazing." For no reason. If anyone else acted enthusiastically about me, I would be embarrassed or annoyed. Not when she does.

In all honesty, what annoys me about my mom is how sympathetic she is toward my father. She isn't sympathetic about my homework and chores not getting done. She is not even sympathetic like that about herself. She is more likely to say she lost her job as a college administrator because of budget cuts and not because my father called eighteen times a day to discuss things.

The joke about Plaster City happened when we were driving across the desert because my mom was going on a job interview at Long Beach State College. Jake and Tess stayed at home with our aunt Debra checking in every three hours. It was my mom's idea of treating them as if they were "responsible decision makers." I think they can handle our being gone a few days. Jake is doing well thanks to his drug-treatment program. Tess has been responsible since she was two hours old, my mom jokes. She says she had to give Tess assignments to break just one tiny rule at the babysitter's. "Don't eat everything on your plate," my mom would suggest. "She could never do it," my mom laughs.

I can't remember why my mother insisted I go with her on the trip to Long Beach. I was not averse. She can make me crazy, but I love being alone with her—especially when we are not talking. Driving at night with her on this trip was pleasant. I got to be in charge of the music; the air conditioning was on, the darkness of the freeway. This closeness with her reminds me of the time we visited the beach, and after I went swimming in the ocean, I got very cold. She put a towel under and over me. Then she took handfuls of really warm sand and poured it over my feet and hands. My eyes were closed, and I heard the ocean sounds. I slipped into this deep enjoyment as if it were both an ancient activity and a private one that only I shared with my mother. Road trips with her could be intimate in the same way.

My mom kept stating facts about the college: "Twenty thousand students. Steve Martin attended and the brother-sister singing duo of the 1970s, the Carpenters. Are these good facts to drop during the interview?" She is mostly talking to herself, not trying to get my opinion, for once, which is good because I don't have one.

As she rattles on, I am having my own thoughts. I like the idea of moving to a beach town. I can imagine myself on the beach. Maybe I would try out for the track team at whatever new school I am at. I can imagine myself on the first day at a new school. What I would do is get a perm; I'd be the new girl with wavy hair. I'd be wearing lipstick and foundation because I will be in seventh grade, and my mom told me I could wear a little makeup once I was in seventh grade.

I would sit in the back of class and slump a little. The problem will come as a result of a writing assignment, I am sure. I love writing, and it causes me embarrassment. The teachers get all excited and cause a fuss. Recently, I won the school writing contest on a "unique perspective." I imagined I was a wedding dress and had served one family through many years and styles. The judges said I excelled at "detail and sound."

I was proud of the essay, but it did cause problems. Mostly attention I did not want. It is also true I asked my mother not to tell my father about the awards assembly. I knew from past experiences that he would dress too exuberantly. For an open house once, he wore a checked coat, a buttoned-down vest, a wide tie and a fedora hat. I don't think it is fair for a girl my age to know what a fedora hat is. Then he asked the teacher how she liked the outfit and went on to explain which thrift store each item came from. One of the annoying factors is he was so there.

Jake and Tess came to the award ceremony for the writing contest I recently won. I didn't mind.

I just did not want a scene. It was just an awards assembly. It was awkward only because my mother wanted to hold my hand. But at least she was sympathetic when I asked her not to; she just said, "Oh, oh, I am sorry."

During the trip to Long Beach, one of the things I figured out was why she will put her sunglasses on at weird times and places: inside the house, at night, especially in the library (another embarrassing thing about my mom is she reads poetry). It is because she cries. The reason I learned this is because we stopped for pie in Yuma, Arizona, and while I went to use the restroom, she put her sunglasses on and called her sister. "I am, I am scared," I caught her saying as I returned and she was wiping her cheek.

Once at night, even before my father was ill, I woke up from a deep sleep. I had heard something; I looked out the window and saw my mom hanging up clothes. She was humming, and her arms were straight up. I loved her so much then, but I knew she would never be mine completely, nor even my father's. She was comfortable with the night, when the whole world is wet with shadows. She was most happy then and got the most comfort. But comfort is different from love. I know she loves me because once when I was five or six, I had heard my father complain about being displaced by me. I remember the look my mother gave him. As if he were speaking in a foreign language; the words were familiar to her but made no sense.

She had special adventures just for me: jumping on the bed, wrestling, she even let me use her as a horse named Joe. My father glared while he pounded out dinner, crab cakes, stir-fry and curry. No food a kid actually likes except for the rice part. But I tried; I let him lecture me about the origins of food. The reason I think I got efficient and good at my homework was because my mom didn't think she could help. Like she wasn't smart enough. "Oh," she would say, "you don't want me doing homework with you. School is your dad's expertise."

I did not like this division of labor, and the homework assistance was problematic. Take the word "drown"—a spelling word I needed to be quizzed on. In my father's hands, the spelling word became a story about a poet who died in a swimming pool near his house when he was young, then a story about my dad being a bad swimmer, then a poem he wrote about almost drowning.

Now that my father is gone, my mom says I have to remember good things about him to keep the good part of my memories alive. She says it is one of the chores I need to do to get my allowance. I can either tell her or draw a picture. Once I drew a picture of my father and me making purple popsicles. We did this every summer. My father did not work; he was a stay-at-home dad. He loved being in the kitchen. He would buy purple Kool-Aid for the popsicles, making my mom mad because of the sugar and stuff. He could have soft eyes too.

Once I told my mom one of my memories was having a sock fight with my father. She looked worried; "Mia, you and I had the sock fights sorting laundry. We played dodge ball in the living room. Mia, that was our game, and you were small. I had to aim for the ankles."

"No," I said, "it was Dad."

She sat on the edge of the couch and looked sad. Then she said, "Oh, dear." Later she went out at night and into the backyard in her bare feet. She looked at the fishpond, where we kept goldfish.

My father stayed at home, and my mother worked at the university. Even in these modern times, this is unusual. It also happened in Leah's family. Sort of. Leah's father sold antiques online and from home. He had one mask over one hundred years old. The mask had straw hair. If you were invited to Leah's birthday party, which I was, twice, her father would at some point put the mask on, and we would squeal and dance and swear it was real. Those were good parties; I enjoyed them.

During this point in our family history, Mom at work, my dad at home and mostly with me because Jake and Tess were in school, my father was very concerned about his father, who lived several states away. At dinner, my mom would ask, "Any luck?" It took me a while to realize they were discussing my father's father. He was homeless, and my father was searching for him. I imagined my grandfather small and hunched. My father found him and brought him back to live with us. He was tall and bald and chubby, which I thought was interesting for a homeless person.

Our grandfather lived with us for two years. My father would take his father to the YMCA, and they would lift weights. I would meet up with them after school. We would get a snack, frozen yogurt or vegetable chips—my mother insisted our snacks be healthy, even if they cost more. My grandfather would talk a little then, but I was not interested. He talked about cars. What I remember mostly during those years was my father was able to keep the kitchen clean. He could cook and clean. I remember because my mother would comment and comment on how impressed she was with his abilities in this area.

My grandfather died while waiting for foot surgery. He choked on food in the hospital, and it was freaky. My mother was outraged; "You need to sue." My father made a few inquiries but never followed through. His cleaning habits changed again. He did corners in the kitchen. But the biggest change was learning his father had left a small estate. A mobile home in Soap Lake, Washington. A cottage at Fort

Ward, Washington. My father started to travel to the Northwest looking for a brother who had gone missing in the Seattle area—turns out he was living with the Snoqualmie Indians. My father wanted to be diligent, making sure property was properly settled and his brother was OK.

They, my parents, argued quite a bit. My mom, I gathered from her talks with her sister with her sunglasses on, was upset because my father did not love his brother but still spent his time looking for him. "Why can't you be with us? You like us, don't you?" She was concerned too. I heard her say to Aunt Debra, "His self-involvement is getting a little loud." He liked to shout poems he had written. He banged pots and pans while he cooked. Things broke accidentally, my great-grandmother's cut-glass bowls.

My father changed toward my brother, sister and me. I had started school. None of us, Jake, Tess or me, took the school bus home. My father picked us up. He swore at traffic after he picked me up from school. He began to yell at all of us and none of us. Once he even swiped at Jake. He started making subversive trips to the fast-food restaurants after school. He bought us fries and a milkshake. We were never hungry at dinner, and that made my mom mad.

The truth of the matter is my father started stealing shortly after his father had passed away. "The love and disease part of the marriage," my mother refers to it now when she is speaking to her sister. It was odd how this was discovered and how I was the agent. Because I was on the honor roll for four years in a row, my parents were eligible for a drawing to win a trip to Ireland. It was a PTA strategy for getting parents involved with their children's school success.

If my mom even remembered the speech given by the principal when I was in kindergarten about an award slated to be given in third grade, I am pretty sure she would not approve. She did not approve of "bribes" for learning.

At the third-grade graduation, the drawing happened— my parents won. Another humiliating moment for me. My mother was literally jumping in the air and high-fiving everyone as she walked up the aisle of the school's gymnasium. I don't blame her for winning, no matter how ironic her victory was. She started planning the trip. My brother, sister and I would trade between my aunt's and Angela's. It was during the planning she discovered the money was missing. She wondered what happened. It was her own account, money her father had left her. My dad admitted he had been writing her name on checks.

Have you ever seen anyone die? My mom's reaction reminded me of this. I remembered visiting my grandfather in the hospital and watching the slowness of the breath and how it gets stuck in the throat and the face looks surprised by the difficulty. My mom's expression exactly; eventually she lifted herself from the couch and walked into the bedroom. Here's how I could tell she was very upset: On the way to the bedroom, she opened the door to the closet where the water heater was. I think she was lost in her own house; she looked like she was trying to figure out where she was.

My father and I were left alone in the living room. He said he was not spending money on bad stuff, just good deals. "Do you want to see?" and he drove me to a storage unit he had rented. "See," he said, "we are prepared for anything." All I can remember is boxes full of canned anchovies and about twenty-two bicycle wheels. I started to cry and asked to go home. He was puzzled and hurt—he was good; he was preparing us. Why did no one see it?

My mom and I slept together the night I told her about the storage unit. Before she got in my bed with me, she knelt beside my bed and made me promise I would never get in the car with my father again. Having your mother cry in the dark while she is kneeling at your bed—it is not anything I would wish upon anyone. Imagine a horse lost at night or a mother cat in a burning house. Imagine some god or religious person making a visitation and asking you to change your life utterly. It was like that.

So much has happened, as you can see. My father says he wants to move back to the Northwest to be with his brother. Perhaps he will be homeless like his father. Perhaps he will miss me and drop in at the library for story hours to see kids and be reminded of me.

What I do know is my mother did not get the job at Long Beach, and I am doomed to be the smartest girl in the class again, next year, one more time.

Jake has a seizure and also becomes a drug addict

I think I might have hated everything from the beginning, even my mom, Joy, with her whispers and fears. Though not so much my father, Frank. He did not stare at me in the dizzying and fearful way Joy did. He would chop vegetables, and I would watch. I liked the fast motion of his wrist and the sound of the knife pounding on the cutting board. I did, I liked it, even as a child.

When I was on drugs, which I have not been for nearly six months, thanks to Intune Intensive Rehab Center, physical motion was altered. I wonder, now, if my father liked to chop so intensely to experience motion differently too. Maybe chopping, like drugs, presented new rhythms so you were able to forget. I got so I needed to forget a lot. Like when I told another lie to someone who cares about me. I needed to forget my problems—the most troubling one, even more than my father's mental health or not having friends, was that I was unable to read because of my dyslexia.

I liked drugs. I am what is called an opportunist. That is, I am not after anything in particular, though there was a little time when I was attached to Percocet. I liked the evenness of the relaxation it provided and the knowledge I would sleep. The bad thing about taking drugs is I hated to disappoint Joy, who always appeared at some point no matter what drug I was on. I felt bad about how stupid she was. I told her anything, and she would believe it. Throughout my life, she would randomly start talking about how some brains like mine needed to stay away from drugs. This was her idea of prevention, to abstractly remind me that my brain didn't function the way other kids' did. Like I might be able to consider that fact when I was offered a free snort of something.

It is hard to speak about my father, how he likes to shop for good deals and how, before he was hospitalized, he would buy me drugs. That was fine once, but now that I am in rehab, I am ashamed. I don't want him to know where I go for rehab. I feel bad about that. He does not deserve my shame. I was egging him on in a way to get me drugs, and he is mentally ill.

Besides, I have this aunt, Joy's sister Debra. She really loves me, and I don't know why. She comes with Joy on family night. She is part of the "parental unit." That is what she and Joy are referred to: "Jake's parental unit." She was there seventeen years ago when I was born; I guess she played a pretty big role because my father passed out during Joy's labor. She gives me these looks like she thinks I am some sort of intricate jewel. She comes with Joy to Intune Rehabilitation when they have family night.

Aunt Debra said the other day, during the sharing part of the evening, that she never knew I was on drugs. Yet when I was younger, she thought it would be so easy to figure it out. She said what hurts her is that she tried to make it clear my whole life that she wanted to be the go-to person for me. That sometimes she thinks I simply rejected her offer.

Then the counselor explained that one of the addict's excellent skills is having no memory. At first, this is vital because when you start as an addict, you can't think about those you are hurting. But, later, there is a neurological reason for the amnesia—when the endorphins start to give way, collapse. Then all the addict cares about is firing up the endorphins, and because of this concern, there is no memory for what can be graceful and fun—the fine feelings when Debra took me fishing or read to me.

There is one strange memory I have. Joy, Debra and I were at a table shucking corn. I must have been eight, but I remember it so clearly. And Joy was saying how Frank was the only man at story hour, the only man at the park. Also that it was OK that Frank didn't work to help with bills because he was fragile and probably had an artistic streak.

Joy said, "I can't begrudge him the messy house and those silly spending sprees at the thrift store."

And Debra said, "Yes, you can begrudge him."

Joy got so mad. First there was this horrible silence and fierce stare. Then she sort of dove into Debra, tackled and wrestled her to the ground and was hitting her and saying, "You are not allowed to say that. This is the family I made; you cannot criticize that."

Boy, Joy was crying, and Debra might have been in shock, and it was my job to pull Joy off, and I did. Then I got each of them water and said, "Let's get back to the shucking." And we did, and that was that.

That family night when Joy was crying and saying,

"Why doesn't he remember how much I love him?" I flashed on that story and thought, *Well, I do have that memory. That childhood memory.* I wondered for a moment if I should repeat that. But decided against it. Maybe that was the beginning of me getting better, knowing the difference between happy memories and those that sting. And being able to resist repeating the sting of that story.

My first memory is waking up screaming, convinced that someone had thrown away my plastic dinosaurs (I had 203 at my peak!). Joy came running in, picked me up and started to open drawers and go through shelves. "See," I remember her saying, "they are still here."

This was not enough. I pointed to all the places I wanted her to look: garbage cans, closets, kitchen cupboards. Then she walked me outside and around the neighborhood to assure me they did not go away to the stars. That part was her idea, not mine. I enjoyed it, though. I needed it; I need overkill.

I also know that I did not have an easy go of it. I was peculiar—there are photographs. Crawling with my butt pointed straight up in the air and no knees bent. That colic hold Joy always points out when we are looking at photos. She is always disheveled in those pictures. She never said anything, but you can see she is worried. About what was never clear. About me? Did she know even when I was young that things were going to go terribly south? Was it because of my father? His craziness just waiting to bloom, and we were the sun and water that fed it?

I know Joy wondered why I had a hard time making friends. I wanted friends, too, but was unable to judge either space or mood. I was always hugging at the wrong time or misunderstanding my friends, thinking they wanted to wrestle or actually wanted me to jump on them. But they didn't. I did it anyway because I thought that was what friends did. I did it because I was furious and because I wanted everything, the allness of my friends.

Though I did enjoy being alone—if being in the imagination and making up stories is alone.

Outside my window, there were bamboo trees, and they could sway, forming shadows on my wall. I would make up stories—that those shadows were ladies. They were hunched, and they were returning. It was late afternoon. From where? Sometimes I imagined a church, a funeral. Who died? One of their sons? Sure. That is how it began, but then I needed to complete the story. To do so, I auditioned different scenarios. The son, he was playing on a green hill. He fell. I always needed to complete the story—while catching butterflies? No, that is too girly. Playing football? No, too boring. Let's see . . . while flying a kite! Still not perfect, but it would do. It gave those shadow women a reason to glide across my wall. After many hours of living with my imagination, I would forget what my vision or idea was. It was like I was making things up in an orderly manner, and then it became crazy and webbed. It was like there was nothing in between order and chaos. I am still that way.

Can I tell you what makes me happy? Nothing. Because I know things, like things never last. In rehab, they say I am supposed to think not about what I want but what others may actually need from me. Or is there anything I can do to not be the center of my universe? It is supposed to be amazing to even just try that.

In fourth grade, for some inexplicable reason, I was

invited to a birthday party in the mall. I remember my parents arguing: Joy thought this was a big deal, and we should buy the gift at the mall, even though she hated the mall. My dad said he saw these really interesting monster figurines at the thrift store. They stood almost up to his knee, and they had grimaces and expressions of anguish and menace. Because my father would not drive Joy to the mall, he won. I have to say that the monster was a big hit, with each kid taking an opportunity to kick it, throw it. Eventually the head was taken off; we all cheered. We had killed the monster!

After killing the monster, eating cake and generally running around, we headed over to the mall, where there was a room with lots of video games. Lots of lights and strange noises. I don't remember anything except for this amazing blue light and then falling. Well, I don't remember if I remember falling. It appeared that I had a seizure. That led to many doctor visits, and I ended up with neurologist visits, landing with a neurologist who said that I must have had a seizure. She said that every person is entitled to two grand-mal seizures before you have to worry. She gave this diagnosis: either I had epilepsy, or it was possible that I was just a weird child. Joy suggested at the dinner table that evening we go with the "weird kid" diagnosis. She thought that between her and Frank, there was enough unusualness to warrant this. My father agreed. He wanted time to pass complacently at all costs.

During this time, my father's father was living with us, and my father was happy and preoccupied.

He bought him and his father lookalike weightlifting gloves, and every morning off they went to the Y. They needed to "lift to live," my father would say. This irked Joy because my father had a difficult time doing other chores for her like taking me to doctors or the library. "It would be too much," he told her.

She would drive me, though she would be checking in at work at the same time. It was kind of sad for me. I knew Joy's urgency in her strained face, but she never spoke to me in the soothing way she did when I was put to bed.

I know I should not, but I resent the many attempts by Joy to cure my dyslexia: tutors that made me memorize face and mouth muscles, basic phonetics and the clay guy. That was "fun." His idea was that I needed to visualize words, not hear them. I made the greatest clay figures to help me remember words: me under a tree with a needle and thread. That was to help me remember the word "so" whenever I saw it on paper. Didn't quite work, though. I blame Joy.

After the clay person, I just gave up and started to listen to loud music. There were years of soothing myself through loud music. Joy didn't understand, but she didn't argue with me. It was the intensity of the hardcore violent chords that got to me, got under my skin. That wasn't the only thing. I liked the lyrics, the generalized "fuck you" that my favorite bands shouted out to all humanity.

Nothing, though, beats drugs. The slow, fuzzy high of pot; the stars of free-basing cocaine; even the slur and aggrandizement of alcohol. I like it all. It is like I had two bodies, and one of those was strictly dedicated to feeling high. This desire was my organizing force. I went to class to score drugs, even went to church. I figured church is supposed to accept everyone, so inevitably someone had ways to get you drugs. This never panned out. At some point, my body, the one dedicated to drugs, became a corpse, and the only way to get rid of the death smell was to use again.

Eventually, even that didn't work. I think because of memory. The remembering it used to be different; it used to be good—like how I used to love swimming underwater and being encompassed in silence or painting with leaves (that was one of Joy's ideas, and she has always been proud of the nuances a mesquite leaf gave a painting). When I was high, I could be possessed by awkwardness and confusion. Music became too slow or screechy or just not as necessary. I began to spend my free time wondering if I was going to have bad confusions when I took my next drug. Or would I avoid thoughts of my adorable little sister, Mia, or dumb Joy? If I did stop to ponder, remorse was right around the corner. God, I hate feeling remorse. After remorse comes the pledge that this will be the last time I get high, but those vows never seemed to work out.

For years, Joy and I have observed a homeless person who appears to loiter where we buy groceries. It's like we have some sort of kinship with him. He rides a bike with a baby trailer. We can never see inside it. Joy thinks it is full of nice clothes. I thought probably just bags with bags inside. Joy and I on occasion buy him a sandwich, and when I got older, I approached him for drugs. He said, "If I had any, they would not go to you." Fair enough.

Joy came home from visiting Sister Joan Clara, this nun she hangs with on occasion. According to Joy, they discuss big questions, and the nun doesn't mind if she cries. Joy's impression of these visits is that she is learning that God does not exist or only exists through prayer and suffering, and somehow that has to be good enough. That doesn't sound like nun talk. But whatever.

One day, Joy said that our "friend" was at the convent, and she learned his name. After my quizzical look, she said, "You know, our homeless guy; we have seen him over by the grocery store."

I nod and ask, "How is our friend, and what is his name, and why was he hanging out with the nuns?"

Joy, I can tell, was happy with my curiosity. She replied, "It turns out that anyone can knock on the convent door and get a bus pass, no questions asked. I asked Sister about him. She told me his name is Ted. I told her I had seen him for many years in town. Ted did not look well today, like maybe he was doing a drug splurge."

She made it sound casual. Does she not understand the desperation of the splurge he is on? How he feels he will die if he doesn't get a fix? Do I explain this desperation? No, I better not. It will send her right back to the nun. The nun will look at her with tolerance, which we family members never quite give her. I decided not to go into detail about what Ted's anguish must be. I don't think Joy can handle it—both emotionally and conceptually. She is so ghostly these days. Her job loss, my drug overdose, and my father's most recent psychotic breaks have turned her into a widow of the living. I don't even know if she knows this, but she is constantly wearing black—black top, skirt and dark, dark sunglasses.

The girls at rehab are pretty cute. One in particular, she is a good friend, a Mormon and a heroin addict. She misses both heroin and church, but I know she is going to get better; someday she will just love church again. I have that kind of faith in her. One of the rules of this rehab place is no relationship with the other clients. I am just flirting anyway.

Before drugs, my father and I had lunch every Saturday (Joy's idea and one of my allowance requirements). I asked him questions about his family. About his uncle Thomas, who would do practical jokes and looked like Khrushchev. That meant my father explained who Khrushchev was, and I impressed my sixth-grade social-studies teacher. A little silly, I think, but I am not going to argue. And I learned about the store that the family owned by the water. I learned about the family cemetery, who was buried there and in what order. I didn't understand it all, but his voice is soothing, and we always went to the best Vietnamese place in town. I learned from my father that he was the one to place his father's ashes in the ground and that he helped carry his grandmother's casket, and it was very light.

One of the reasons I am sad and angry is because no one knows why I am different. Why my dyslexia is the most severe any teacher has ever seen. Or if I will ever have the seizure that the neurologist says I am entitled to—and what would that mean, anyway? I have these females—Joy; her sister; my sisters, Tess and Mia—they all worry about me. It drives me mad and makes me feel bad—I do not care back as strongly as I should.

Sometimes late at night, I look at the stars and try to imagine what my seizure was like those many years ago. I imagine many stars moving fast through me so that my body existed but only vaguely. Sometimes I wonder what it will be like to never use drugs again. The reason I like the idea of never using drugs is strange because it lets my sadness be real—that the sadness is based on the facts of my life and not the hallucinations that move in with drugs.

The other day, Joy said, "I kind of like being a rehab family. I mean, it is not easy, but at least I have a clue of what's going on, which I did not have when you were using." Joy having a clue, I admit that kind of made me laugh when I thought about it. It was late at night; I was smoking a cigarette, and the smoke went straight up but did not quite reach the sky. Smoke rising, Joy getting a clue, and it is just about good enough.

Tess has tea with Bobbie, Bobbie and Susie

I am annoyed, can be annoyed, will be annoyed, have been annoyed, etc. Notably at my mom, whom my brother calls Joy, which she never corrected. Then when he was age fifteen, she said, "Hey, I want to be called Mom." Good luck with that one.

This is not to say I don't adore and crave her. She reminds me of the new and fancy whiteboard they have in the classroom, where instead of chalk they use computers and draw numbers or bring up stories from the Internet; it is electrifying but also very easily malfunctions. I do go to her, and she listens no matter what. Sometimes it is about family and sometimes about friends. I know that she has no idea what I am talking about, like when I ask, "What are the genetics of my nose?" but she doesn't let on she doesn't know; she will ask questions or pretend answers ("I think the family nose took a turn during the potato famine"). That is what I like about her; she does not get me, but she does absorb me.

Here are two things that interest and annoy me about my mom: she feels sorry for the strangest people, and there are some things she is absolutely clueless about. Once these two characteristics collided but, I have to admit, to my advantage. What happened was this woman came to our house and was selling homemade dolls. This woman had no teeth, and her calves were large. She explained that Melinda had sent her to my mother. Of course, Melinda with liver spots and a limp.

Let me tell you about Melinda. Not sure how she arrived and became so constant in our lives. She was another one of my mother's causes. I think originally my mother met her at work. Melinda was a talker. Mostly about her longstanding ailments. Her cleft foot, for instance. She could not quit talking about her klept foot and the burden because of it. I have to say that I liked and still do like Melinda and her largeness. I still see her; my mom still has her over. Melinda will sit there and talk about her illnesses, and we all stare at her, my mom especially. We are mesmerized by her—her voice, her continuous list of problems. Melinda has constant problems. My family has an impressive list of problems—loss of job for my mom, a final break with reality for my father and, of course, Jake. Jake and his drug-abuse history.

Anyway, this woman came to our house, to our door. When my mom answered, with me at her side, we heard the woman explain that Melinda sent her. I cannot remember this woman's name—remember I was only five, compared to the fifteen that I am now.

Now here is the clueless part regarding my mom. At that point in my history, I only had one doll, Susie. I am not sure how I got her. Susie had problems. I am not sure what I had done to her clothes, but she was naked all the time. Also I had painted her face blue and had cut her hair. But my mom had never seemed to notice. She never asked questions or scolded me. She seemed to accept that Susie was that way by design, not by my damage.

So I was a little surprised when I saw she was agreeing to buy two dolls. Up until this point, she did not ever show any indication that dolls were something a young kid might want. Though when I saw the stranger at the door, it made sense—even more when I saw what the dolls looked like: each with mop heads for hair, stuffed rags for a face and body. My mom would be willing to get dolls, but they would have to be weird, and they would have to be from a weird person that she was supposedly helping. My mother purchased the dolls and closed the door.

"Here," my mom said, holding the doll out so that it nearly touched the tip of my nose. "What do you want to call her?"

"Bobbie," I said.

As years went by, my mom would describe the next moment as "adorable." What happened next is my mom handed me the second doll, saying again, "Here. What do you want to call her?"

The doll looked nearly the same as the doll I'd just named. I guess with my "bowl-haired" seriousness, I thought for a moment and said, "Bobbie."

"You want to name them both Bobbie?"

"Yes."

"OK," said my mom.

I think my mom was confused about what to do next. So after a bit of silence, she said, "Do you want to have a tea party with Bobbie and Bobbie?"

I remember asking, "Can Susie come?"

"Of course she can."

My mom had this way of acting like she knew what she was doing. She acted with authority when I knew she felt none. I like that, I admit. She scoured my room. Suddenly she spotted my plastic hamper and turned it upside down. "A table," she announced. She grabbed a towel and asked me to put the tablecloth on, and I did, and with my own pretend authority, I placed four small chairs around the table.

Then my mom got the look, I know it well, part panic and part prayer. I never knew and still do not know what to do with that look. Am I supposed to worry? Am I supposed to leave her alone? What I did that time was ask for a teapot.

"Of course," she said. Then she did something I never expected of her. She went to the locked cupboard and took off the lock with a key she had with her car keys. This cupboard used to be opened only once a year at Thanksgiving and only by my parents. However, two years ago, my parents had a fight. He accused her of having middle-class taste. She cried and locked the cupboard. It had never been opened since.

She took down the Spode china teapot and matching cups and saucers for all of us. She filled the teapot with water and put Cheerios and chocolate chips in two little bowls. That is when we both realized that there were only four chairs—one short. My mom said she would sit on the ground. And she did. She folded her legs underneath her, and we commenced the very first tea party with Bobbie, Bobbie and Susie.

It was my mom who started to talk in a high-pitched voice. I think it was her idea of a rich old person. "I flew to England this morning to try to get Bobbie, Bobbie and Susie matching dresses, but they did not have the right sizes. So I hope you don't mind, but I got them goats instead." OK, this sort of seemed familiar. I mean, my mom was capable of being silly, pillow fights and flying angels.

"Goats?" I asked. "What do you mean by goats?"

"Well," she said, using the voice again. "Well, they are mostly white, and Grouch has a blue bell, and William has freckles in his eyes. Oh, dear, I only bought two. What shall I do?"

"Maybe Bobbie, Bobbie and Susie could practice sharing?" I offered, using my version of a grown-up voice.

"Excellent," my mom replied.

"Where will they sleep?" I asked.

"I am going to build them a room out in the backyard; it will be made out of hay. If you agree, we can toast to that." With that, my mother lifted the Spode china teacup and said in a whisper, "Toast."

As I lifted my cup, she continued to whisper, "Very carefully. This was your great-grandmother's, Carol Lynch. I found it in shoe boxes in her house after she died and I was cleaning. I asked my mom, her daughter, and your grandmother if I could keep the china. My mom didn't see that it would be a problem because, after all, she was supposed to send it back to Ireland many years ago but never got around to it, so there was no real home for it. Let's be careful with it," whispered my mom in her normal voice.

"OK," I whispered back, and we clinked our cups softly.

Then I started whispering. I whispered that Bobbie, Bobbie and Susie had been arguing about the best songs written. That Bobbie and Bobbie really liked the song "Brown-Eyed Girl," and Susie was in favor of anything Michael Jackson sang. I let on to my mom that I didn't know what to do and that everyone was unhappy and fought. She asked if I had ever thought of writing a song that combined the tunes. No, I had not.

She took out a sheet of paper and said why didn't I try making one song from the two songs. I was excited; this meant a solution and an opportunity to perform. I picked up a spoon as a microphone and began to sing while my mother wrote the words to my song: "Brown-eyed girl / she's mine / standing in the sunshine / singing a simple melody . . . " I paused and paused some more. Then: "Singing in a rainstorm / like A-B-C, as easy as . . . "

I could think of no more, so I bowed. My mom stood up and clapped and shouted, "Bravo!" Sometimes my mother knows what to do. I see that sometimes. In addition to the songs, she also seemed to know that we were going to ignore the fact that Bobbie and Bobbie were mopheads. "One thing I do know about Bobbie and Bobbie is that we should never try to comb their hair. In fact, let's drink to that. Gently." We lifted our Spode china and tinked them together once again.

I wanted to ask her to tell me a story because I did not want the tea party to end. But I had to weigh out that request: If I asked for a story now, would I give up the option for one that evening ? Our bedtime stories were cool because my mom let me tell her the characters I wanted and where the location would be. I always wanted the story to take place on the roof of our house and to include my cousin Liz, who was very blond. In the stories, Liz could twirl from the roof, or she could fly. Other times, Liz did a jazz dance with our dog, Lucky. I did not want to miss out on that.

She seemed to know what I was thinking. In her normal voice—oh, I have to say this: Her voice is angelic. One of the confusing things about my mother is no matter how sad or angry, she sounds sweet and kind. She started to tell a story about the first year her family moved to this desert town because of her brother's asthma. The winter was much milder than it was in Chicago. Nonetheless, Joy's mother special-ordered a coat from Niemen Marcus. Though beautiful, it was a nuisance for my mother—the coat got in her way. She constantly needed to take it off and look for a place to store it. She was pretty good at remembering where she had stashed it, but once she left it in church after a school rosary session for an ailing nun. Joy didn't realize it was gone until after dinner. Terrified, she confided in her brother—he was seventeen and successfully monitoring his asthma. They came up with a plan. Joy would go to bed, and her brother, Jim, would say he was running an errand. He would retrieve the coat and slip it to Joy through a bedroom window.

Everything was fine. Joy went to bed, and while kneeling for her prayers, her mother came in and asked, "How's the coat?" Joy remembered thinking to herself, *What an odd phrase.* As if the coat had a life.

"Fine," Joy replied, a little puzzled.

"Can I see it?" her mother asked. "I love the material."

It was then that Joy had to tell the truth: the coat was left in church, and Jim had gone to retrieve it.

While telling this story to me, my mom began to wonder out loud why she didn't attempt to divert the subject or simply lie. It was kind of like I wasn't there. She wondered out loud why she was always so obedient. It wasn't necessarily a good thing. "Tess, you can be little dishonest, especially if you are a child and your dignity counts on it." That was the end of the story.

What I learned later from my uncle Jim, before he died, was that Joy was beaten that night. It was the first time, and there would be two other times before Joy was fifteen, and after that there would be no more. Joy was stunned as her mother wept and said, "I could have been someone who shopped at good department stores, but instead I am here."

Jim arrived, finally, with the coat. He said he peeled their mother away and walked her into the living room and quietly handed her over to his father. Jim was furious and wanted nothing to do with her. He went back to Joy and stroked her hair.

The question I ask but have no answer to is, Where was my father during teatime? There were only a few options: he was sleeping, shopping or walking around the mall with his father for exercise. Sometimes I felt my father loved me even better than my mom. He was proud of me and would take me to meet store clerks and would make up songs about me using Woody Guthrie lyrics. Instead of "I am sticking to the union," it would be "I am sticking to the Tess girl till the day I die." I would dance to his tunes. It was just there was no predicting with him. At least he wouldn't get furious with me—that I always knew. He would just talk nonsense sometimes. And always about himself. What a great deal-finder he was. And probably that he was an amazing poet. And, if truth be told, the smartest one in this "whole household." Somehow I didn't think that he should say those things. That it might hurt my mom's feelings, but I wasn't sure. After all, he was my father, and he was talking that way, and that made it be right, right?

I asked my mom if we could toast again, though there was no real reason to. Yes, my mom said, and we did. I knew the tea party was over. I was sort of sad because my mom had told a sad story and seemed saddened by it. But she said, "Thank you for inviting me to this tea party. I hope we can do it again soon." That was typical too. The tea party was her idea, not mine, but she didn't like to be the idea person around kids. It was like she thought it made her a bad mom.

We did have more tea parties with Bobbie, Bobbie and Susie. Always the same setup: turned-over plastic hamper for a table, a towel for a tablecloth, but never again with the Spode china. After the first tea party, it was paper cups. That part I remember. That and how we always found a reason to make a toast. Thinking back on those tea parties, there was not one in which I can place my father as a guest or even a presence in the house. How disloyal have I been, then? To love him and love his absence? To feel at home with Bobbie, Bobbie and Susie. Even today, with him gone from our lives, there are many things I imagine saying to bring him back. But describing those sweet, sweet parties is not one of them.

When I visited him in the last psychiatric hospital, we were sitting at a square table in the cafeteria. He was telling us about his day and the talks on brain function during stressful family fights. How you could breathe properly and change everything. For some reason, that made me think of Bobbie, Bobbie and Susie. I had to breathe for all of them, didn't I? And I did, and I celebrated them with a toast. And when I put my teacup down, it was always with an exhale.

Joy learns her husband has been stealing and other things too

Money was always a problem. Frank did not work. I was never sure why, and I don't think Frank knew either. Here are some of the reasons we gave ourselves and others: Frank took care of the children; he needed to be able to see his sick father; he was going to work soon; he hated applying. He did apply, didn't get the job. He got sad; I got a raise; what was the use?

In spite of having a master's degree in administration and being a whiz at discussing economic theory, especially Marxism, he couldn't manage the finances of our house. Besides, I wanted a lot: a special neurologist for Jake, an enlightened daycare for Mia, Saturday enrichment classes for Tess.

Afterschool programs, dinner out—actually, no dishes to clean, to be precise.

Why didn't Frank work? It would have helped, it might have, I speculated while doing the despair lounge. I loved the shadows the cactus made. He didn't work because he loved his fear more than me, I said to myself. I wanted it to be about me. But it was not. He was fractured; he was sick, mentally ill. *Hiding that was the most important thing we did*, I thought to myself. And, finally, we didn't do that, hide, at all.

When Frank would become depressed and withdrawn, he ignored me and put me off. He said "maybe," but never "no," to any inquiry I might make, from "Are you making dinner?" to "Do you want to seek medical help?" When would he have an answer? That is what gnawed me always. It was like living from dusk to night. Dusk can be beautiful and magnanimous with its various colors. At first, it is intriguing: You wonder about what is to come. But eventually, and sadly, the dusk, the sky of possibilities, always brings darkness.

Before we left for this crazy trip to Ireland, I had discovered Frank had been writing my name on checks from an account with only my name on it. I had money from my father there and was sentimental about those funds, as if money could be that way, really. It was a gift my father left for me in his will. I wanted to use the funds in ways that would please my father. In my mind, that meant the money was about the children and their so-called enrichment. Frank believes that enrichment is bourgeois and that I probably would agree if I were not so bourgeois myself. But initially he agreed with my sentiment about my father's gift in a patronizing sort of way.

At some point, however, reserved Frank decided the account could be accessible to him as long as it was used on good deals. He never discussed this with me. I learned later that he didn't talk to me about this because I was so middle class, and that confounded his working-class shame. Besides, he was trying so hard to have the family prepared for all possibilities. His purchases were not extravagant or deviant, just nonsensical: broken chairs, broken bike parts, good deals at the grocery outlet (a case of canned anchovies!) and new thrift-store wardrobes for all.

I sought the advice of two people on how to handle my new knowledge that Frank had been taking money from this account: my friend Angela and my brother Michael. Angela and I grew up together and were college roommates. Angela was not always my go-to friend because for many years her attitude toward Frank was "just do not tolerate that." But like all of us, Angela softened after she experienced loss. For Angela and her husband, Tom, it was losing a baby in infancy and then waiting so long for their son, Jules, to arrive. Now she listens and simply says, "What can I do for you?"

I went to Angela because I needed clarity. She specializes in clarity. Her life is clear. One that involves allowing simple and direct looks over your shoulder at the past and then straightening up and moving forward. But Angela was stymied too. How does someone you love steal from you? Neither of us had experience with this. I was inclined to feel guilty. I pleaded to Angela, "But there has to be a cause and effect here. I just know it." I was thinking something like my class background, though not extraordinary, was more comfortable than Frank's difficulties being raised by adults whose focus was simply on surviving, food and heat. Who found a kind of desperate happiness with inebriations, loud songs and good fishing days. Perhaps I demanded too much, and therefore Frank sought his own terrain of control.

Angela just said, "Shut the fuck up with that. That's bullshit. Stealing is stealing." Then she said, "What can I do for you?" and I said, "Hmm." As I was contemplating, she started to laugh, and I asked what was so funny. She reminded me that when she tried to advise me not to marry Frank, I said, "Why? What could go wrong?" She admitted that she and her husband often referred to me as "Joywhatcouldgowrong."

OK, this made me laugh, and I said, "Obviously what I had was a failure of imagination."

My brother Michael received more details from me than Angela did. I told him Frank had a storage shed where he kept his accumulated junk. That he had been taking money. That the house really had no order and that I had no idea what to do and lacked even the imagination to comprehend this set of behaviors. Michael asked questions like "What else did he hide?" "Did he sleep quite a bit after a shopping spree?" "How was his eye contact?" Michael gave me the name of a psychiatrist. The only person who was not told was Debra, my sister. All these years, I had to protect Frank from Debra's disapproval. I know that Debra loves me the way a cougar loves its young. I was not prepared for Debra's anger toward Frank.

At the psychiatrist's office, Frank began to speak quickly, began to say he took the money because of a false attachment to his mother as a young one; he acted disoriented. He also sputtered about keeping his father alive, rescuing his dad from his destiny as a homeless person. He was not sure I understood the bravery and power in that. It was about taking care of us, all of his family. That is what his secret purchases were and the shed. There was no malice. I knew there was no malice in his acts, but that only helped me feel worse somehow.

The psychiatrist said quietly, "You must get to a hospital. Your behavior is manic." There was no place to take him because he was not homicidal or suicidal enough. Next best was intensive daily appointments. Much to Frank's chagrin, the intensive treatment seemed to be more about medicine than opportunities to explain his erratic behavior. Luckily, I thought, and yet knew I was being unhelpfully romantic here, Frank wanted to blame his behaviors on class and economics and not on my failure to love in the right way. Because who does know how to love the right way? That is, with a passion designed to remove genes and bad behavior. It seems like just once in a lifetime we should get a free pass and be allowed our hubris. That we would not be slapped down for wanting and trying to make things different. I still wish I could love away Frank's genetic proclivities, his class distress and his social malfunctions. Just that one pass to love it away. Why was that so wrong? It remains my greatest disappointment that my love made no difference in Frank's behavior. My love did not cause his neurons to trigger differently. My second level of disappointment was that Frank's decisions were not about love or even the economics of class. His rationale had to do with protecting and being prepared for some great disaster. He did not see that we, he and I, our family were the disaster we needed protection from.

After a month of daily visits to a psychiatrist, a plan was hatched. I found Frank a small one-room cottage about a mile from the house, so the children were close to him; I thought that would make everyone happy. I agreed to stay married—I loved him; I was Catholic; wouldn't it be best, somehow, for the children?

Sometimes I would come home from work, those first few months, and he would be sitting on the front porch.

There was an aura of disorganization around him. He never accepted my invitations to come in, though it was fall and the sun was setting early, bringing with it coolness. He said, "Could I just sit here on your porch?"

I started to hate his ghostly approach and could not decide if it violated my principle of the "reorganized family." Frank chose this approach—I had agreed to a continuation of the family, not his casting an autumn shadow over our daily routines. I decided that I would try to ignore him. The children nodded to him, too, when they arrived home from school. With Frank sitting on the front porch, I attempted as much as I could to continue with his shadowy presence. I fed the kids Cheerios, cheese, cucumber slices and apples. He never made a fuss or asked for anything. When it was dark, Frank would leave his chair, knock on the living-room window and wave goodbye. Sometimes before leaving, he would call me over to a window and ask me to open it.

He would say to me about our youngest child, Mia, "As long as she can skip, I don't have to die." Was this a veiled suicide threat? Was he not getting the right medicine? Was I able to care?

I would call my brother Michael and ask, "Do I care?"

Michael would say, "You are going to try not to. You are going to ask yourself, 'What do the children need?'"

The first few times we had this conversation, I would say, "I don't know what the children need."

And Michael would say, "Is there milk in the house? Is there clean laundry? Do the children have homework? Do you need to help them with that?"

"Oh, I get it," I replied. And I did. I got so I was good

at always having milk in the house and the kitchen dishes cleaned.

After talking to Michael, I realized that I had not yet turned on the lights in the house. All the rooms were dark, except the kitchen light, where we ate my mediocre meals and squabbled with each other. Never mentioning Frank. I would turn the lights on as we were preparing for bed and then slowly turn them off after the doors were closed behind each child.

Later, I would admit to Angela and eventually Debra that I could not place the children those first days and months of the family's reorganization. I know that I prepared the oddest meals, tomatoes and mayonnaise, chocolate and carrots. I know that I started the concept of girl beds. Mia and Tess would join me on the king-size bed. I said it was for warmth and to save money on the electric bills. But this went on longer than it should have.

I had changed routines, habits, to accommodate my lethargy in loss. I explained to Angela and Debra once when we were eating by candlelight at Angela's that I loved my despair lounges but had to limit them. They both asked, "What is a despair lounge?" I realized that these were of my own making and were not a signature for normal life.

I explained, "The exercise of lying in bed, with ankles crossed, staring out the window, a large prickly pear outside making wonderful shadows and forming a natural curtain." They looked at me as if I was crazy. While reaching for the mussels, I said in my own defense, "I managed to make my own coffee . . . I think." We laughed. Perhaps it is for these moments that we suffer. To realize the sky is exquisite and laughter gravity.

Before I moved him out of the house, while he was stealing, he cooked and cleaned but not both. He was irritable with the children. Picking them up from school was particularly horrible; I gathered that from listening to the children. The children would fight with each other, and Frank would get involved. Tess would later explain, "Dad was swiping at the air, at us, though he never hit us, not really." Frank would take them to McDonald's. I guessed later that he might have been trying to give his mind a break. It must have been filling up slowly with ongoing chatter.

Before the final crack, the chaos at home, always present, became even more evident. The floors covered with paper, couches with food; once, dishes in the laundry cabinet. He didn't seem to notice. A hostile air loomed. He was angry but cooking. He was trying to calm himself down with stir-frying and ethnic spices. We were holding their lives together, not knowing they were swimming in its demise.

I knew he suffered the travails of the housewife. But his isolation must have been even worse than any housewife he came across at the park or story hour, where he was the only male and so suspect. It was his narcissism that probably got the better of him and did not allow him to reach out to others. Besides, we were very busy with the fictions we needed to maintain: "We like our lives. We aren't lonely in our skin. The house is OK messy. What is wrong with unswept clutter in the middle of the floor?"

I used to write in the closet every morning. A "closet poet," Angela would laugh at me. Then ask, "Why don't you get a desk?" How could I explain how I liked to be huddled in a corner, how silent it was in the closet, how amazing to have no audience, for this moment, this one moment? However, on occasion, Tess would join me there. She would sit quietly in front of me and stare. I thought years later I should have kicked her out. It would have been good for us. But I didn't. Instead, I let her sit and watch—her bowled brown hair and freckles. Tess became and remains a jealous and brilliant lover. She has demanded to know why I had others in her life, demanded to know the real status of Santa Claus.

Here are some of the things I told her: "I don't know why I longed for others." "I don't know Santa's true status, in all honesty." Then, finally, which I had no business saying, "Because the world never provides enough, and, eventually, even the imagination betrays us. So we look for others."

Frank and I went to Ireland our last summer together. I had not yet lost my job. My favorite place was Ardmore, where my grandfather was from. We had a large room on the ocean, a church across the way; perhaps my grandfather was baptized there? There were long stretches of beach and a trail into the cliffs, dramatic and dangerous. This is the place where Saint Declan was baptized. Saint Declan gave sight to the sick as an emissary of Christ and is considered the true founder of Christianity in Ireland.

There was a shrine to Saint Declan on the top of the cliffs. It was here I determined that Frank's stealing was my fault and a direct result of me not taking charge of my own money. I decided to give Frank a budget for groceries and gas. That would solve our problems; if Frank managed those two things and I did everything else, we would be fine. I am not sure why, but this made me elated. I ran back to the room and woke Frank. He said the "no/maybe" thing. But

I ignored him; we were on the verge of happiness. Early the next morning, it rained. Plings hitting the rooftops—rain and roof in a kind of duet. We listened, and made love.

Two months later, back in the desert, my anxiety was back. Weight gain, I guessed. One morning, I jumped into the car to go exercise. I ran out of gas, walked home, borrowed Jake's bike, got gas, rode the bike to the car, put gas in the car, put the bike in the car, took the car to get filled up, got to work on time. That night, I woke Frank and told him he would need to move out. "I know," he said.

1986
Joy makes history

It was shockingly typical in many ways. I was flattered when Mark, my favorite literature professor, called and asked me out. I drank too much, let myself be convinced I was beautiful, when, at best, I knew I was just unusual-looking. I let myself be walked into the bedroom, undressed. And in the dark and with my eyes tightly closed, as a way of attempting to not be where I so clearly was, I let myself be convinced that it was OK to "do this." I was partly flattered, partly determined to get the night over with. I knew that Mark would only leave after sex. He made that part clear.

Yet we continued our affair during the final days of summer. Mark would be leaving soon, going on a sabbatical to teach at the University of Shanghai with his girlfriend, a graduate student in philosophy. For the rest of my life, I would wonder what compelled me to such actions, besides stupidity and loneliness. Loneliness and stupidity could describe anyone at some point in their lives; most find a way to get off that train wreck of self-inflicted wounds. Not me.

He was almost my type. Tall and chiseled, a fondness for plaid, though it was the 1980s, and khaki and corduroy would have been more appropriate for a literature professor. I assumed he must have respected my writing, especially my paper on "The Silences in Jane Austen's Drawing Rooms." "Wow," is the only thing he wrote on the paper, next to a grade of A+.

I had demonstrated that the silences in *Pride and Prejudice* were required for the artist writing the novel and for the characters. Jane Austen herself tackled her work secretively in the evenings during parlor games, hiding her writing underneath sheets of musical scores. Silences also allowed the characters to be examined in stereo. Darcy is more Darcy as he impatiently listens to poor singing. It is his impatience that allows the reader to speculate that he cannot tolerate what is genuine and, therefore, is not a good match for the intelligent, lively, and real Catherine Bennett. I made my case with a great many quotes from Austen's novel as if to say, "Don't trust me; trust the author."

Mark had a reputation for being a diverse and sensitive reader of contemporary fiction. He was kind to female characters, and once, to my fascination, publicly scolded one of my classmates for saying the main character in Kate Chopin's book was hysterical.

However, I was the one who was diligent about birth control. He did not seem to take it as seriously. I thought this might have something to do with his age. He was more than twenty years older and came of age in the early 1960s— in between *Playboy* and the sexual revolution. This plagued him as he tried to be a sensitive swinger. It made him less than real.

We both knew the affair would be short-lived. Mark would be leaving soon, off to teach American literature to

Chinese students. Mark, I believe, was hoping our affair would once again ignite his longing for his girlfriend, Renee. Their relationship, he said, was no longer in his grasp. Something he could no longer touch. Renee was younger than he and had taken up marathon running. Mark, I gathered from his openness in speaking about her, was dismayed at her self-sufficiency and bossiness. He was not sure why or if he was needed. He could not get Renee interested in asking him why he left on Wednesday afternoons. He wanted her to be interested. He wanted to need to lie about those two hours he spent with me. But Renee would simply shout out the door as he left, "Can you pick up some chicken livers and red wine on your way home?"

It was a guilt or ennui, then, that allowed us to continue our affair with the knowledge that it had a built-in end. However, almost immediately, I began to find Mark's visits vaguely painful while also compelling. They were like a sore tooth that I continued to touch because I was intrigued by the discomfort. He was boring if he was not talking about literature. He was inexperienced; this sabbatical was the first time he would leave the country. I thought about Flannery O'Connor's statement that to be a writer, one must leave home, either in one's imagination or quite literally. Mark did not appear to have left home, making me wonder why O'Connor's statement was true for writers but not readers of literature. How could Mark be such a brilliant reader and yet such a boring person?

Yet I felt hopeful, somehow, by the clear path Mark's life took. I was happy that clear paths existed. His only unpleasant discussion with his family was his career choice. I would listen with some interest as he spoke about disappointing his father by not going into business. I knew I should admire his courage but never quite mustered the proper sympathy for his career difficulties. He had gone from home to college to graduate school to teaching. He had married once, for a short time. No children, luckily, he would say. He didn't have affairs with students until he was approached by one and then other female students. He had a rule and always said no to undergraduates but yes to graduate students. He made an exception with me on the speculation that I was a little older than most undergraduates.

I once asked, "Have you ever had to be a waiter?"

"No, why would I?" he asked, baffled.

Well, I wondered out loud and very sincerely, perhaps he needed the money or had a crush on a waitress? It was an odd question, I thought later, trying to figure out why I asked it. Maybe it was an effort to make him more real. To ground these afternoons with something banal but solid, like work, like history.

He did have a crush on the waitress at the country club his family belonged to. He was fifteen, and she may have been twenty-one. Once, she snuck him a martini, and they ended up making out on the golf course that evening. But this did not require him to be a waiter, he offered.

I began a contest with myself to determine what his Midwest and young complications and challenges were. "Hey," I would ask, almost casually, so as to not reveal the internal game I had invented, "did you ever buy your own car?" Another odd question, I guess. Was I hoping for stories of backseat sex? Illicit trips to whorehouses? What exactly was I after? I never really knew. A way out of my boring life, which was becoming more and more frightening to me? I still needed to borrow money to live. I, too, studied literature because I was good at it, not necessarily passionate. I drank too much.

Supposedly, I wrote poems that were compelling but could never follow through with those editors who offered to help me "get going." I thought that my "gift" of poetry writing, as one editor described it, was embarrassing. Though I did believe in poetry more than anything, I did not know how to fight for it. Or I was unwilling to fight for it. Ennui, again. I must have had a great deal in common with Mark.

"No," Mark replied to the inquiry about the car. "I have been urban. My whole life. I have lived in cities and never learned to drive. I took public transportation."

"Urban?" I queried. "Like museums and existential cafés for existential poetry readings?"

"Well, yes, but I preferred bookstores and libraries." He laughed a little. "They were easier to get to and transported me quicker than poetry."

Alcohol was perhaps where our lives diverged. Mark's father was a silent and steely drinker. My mother was boozy and unpredictable. I endured occasional parental beatings from my mother. Once, my mother came to me in the middle of the night and woke me up to express her sloppy and drunken fears that I was just not beautiful. Usually, she was not so direct as she was standing over my bed that night. Usually, she would say with a hopeful and helpful tone, "It is not that you are unbeautiful, dear, but your beauty has not found you yet. You will have to grow into your nose, and if only I could get you to lighten your hair."

Once, though, later, my mother woke me up. Perhaps I was seventeen. She slurred, "Dear, dear, it has dawned on me, you are beautiful. You are unusual, you are, you are, Roman-looking." From that moment on, my mother would look at me gently and say, "You are so beautiful." This only served to make me even more awkward and fearful around her. And to question the strange motivations of my mother. Why was the state of my beauty so important anyway?

When I discovered I was pregnant, I hated both myself and Mark. I hated myself and my stupid arrogant games that allowed me to feel superior to him because life was rougher for me. Where did it get me, what did it achieve? I hated him for being boring and yet causing this life-altering direction to me, to my body. I hated him because in spite of my luke-warm feelings toward him, I made love. I hated him for being the vessel that carried, hand delivered to me, my own self-hate. I had no money, no affections, no desire, and yet there it was, a baby attached to my uterine wall, dying to grow.

"How could that be?" I asked the nurse in Student Health, thinking of how careful I had been with the dia-phragm. The nurse looked back at me like I was a Martian. "I mean, I have always used birth control."

"Sometimes it happens," the nurse responded. "Absti-nence is the only foolproof method."

I had an urge to hit the nurse. But instead I said, "What do I do now? How does one schedule an abortion?" I took the information down. The nurse offered that student insur-ance would cover this, and because abortion had been legal for nearly twenty years, practitioners would be easy to find, but so would protestors. I wondered, *Is this person really sanctimonious, or am I imagining it?* I remembered the excruciating lectures the nuns gave about hygiene and the importance of covering up the smell of one's menses.

I took the information down from the nurse and marched across campus to Mark's office. It was odd to feel this anger and passion; I had been dulled for so long. My energy only added to my sputtering anger. I was disoriented with many unspecified feelings. I stormed into Mark's office. It was the first time I had been there as his lover. Before, I was his student, trying to figure out what would give me a good grade and later to discuss and gather his support for my graduate-school application. Of course he would support it, I remember him saying. I was relieved and surprised by that.

I closed the door behind me and told him that I was pregnant. I looked outside at the ledge of his window. It was covered with pigeon shit. Why did I never notice that before? He looked at me looking at the pigeon debris. He was trying to rearrange the information and make this news go away. Mark said, "Disgusting, huh? They clean it once a year for family weekend, but it is appalling again within a week after the cleaning."

I said that I was not going to blame him, but I expected him to take his fair share of responsibility and to help this be taken care of. He wondered out loud if that meant I wanted him to find more waivers for me to pay for graduate school the following fall. Or a more prestigious scholarship than the one I received. "Because if you do," he said, "I cannot. It would be unethical, and besides, all the money has been given out. Also, I would need to discuss this, your demand for money, with my department chair."

I looked at him and seethed. "Listen, did you hear what I just said? This has nothing to do with literature. This is not some parlor scene. We, yes, we have a disaster."

Mark put his arms up as if he were not interested in

fighting arrest but also genuinely confused about how he was supposed to help. He was a professor; he was preparing for a sabbatical; he had a personal commitment to his girl-friend. It was casual between us. Though we never discussed it as such, we both knew that. "I have had many affairs, not as many as some of my colleagues, but I have been careful enough," Mark said self-righteously. "I have always asked my partners if they were using birth control. No one had ever gotten pregnant before. I am preparing for a sabbatical. Look, I am sorry. I am trying to get out of here. I leave in three weeks. What can I do for you?"

What can you do for me? I thought. You can turn the clock back and quit existing. You can make those lukewarm afternoons go away. You can make Jane Austen someone who never existed. *It was her fault I met you,* I thought. What I said was, "Give me three hundred dollars to help with the abortion costs."

"I can't afford that. Besides, if I wrote you a check, Renee would be suspicious."

I asked, "Who is Renee?"

Mark said, "My girlfriend."

Until that moment, she did not have a name. I was pretending that she did not exist. The horribleness of my boredom was multiplying. I was getting angrier and angrier as I began to think of Renee. Yet I tried to muster my indig-nation again and said, "Now, why would I care about that?"

"Hey, listen," Mark replied, "why the sudden aggression? It's not like you were not aware of the possible consequences of your actions."

"Fuck you," I said. "Give me one hundred dollars." He wrote out the check. I left.

I bought a bottle of wine. I drew a bath. I looked outside the window at the mountains. I remembered that my mother, once drunk, told me that when she learned she was pregnant with me, her fourth child, she took to swimming in the ocean. She hoped "the rough waves would do what the rhythm method did not." "What a fucked destiny," I thought. "I am a failure at living and not dying. What kind of purgatory does that put me in?" But when I started to weep, it was for Renee. Renee, the marathon runner, the philosophy student. Renee, someone who had a plan for life.

I learned later that Mark would complain about me to the chair of the department, that I might be a stalker. In truth, I am not a stalker. I am not passionate enough. And the chair liked me; he said so once while he was in his cups at a party for the scholarship students like me. I knew also from that one boozy conversation with the chair that Mark was a disappointment. "A promising scholar," the chair said, "but Mark never wrote again after his first book on American theater in the last half of the nineteenth century." Mark was kept because he was a good teacher. And for some inexplicable reason, feminists liked him. "Mark is adequate," the chair said, "and I am happy to see Mark leave for a year. Perhaps it will incite him to take up his work again and in a serious manner."

Joy tells Sister Joan Clara some of the things she wants

Sometimes I wondered what name I would have taken if I had become a nun. I wondered this on my walk to see Sister Joan Clara, whom I visited almost every Thursday. I assumed that Sister Joan Clara took her name to honor Joan of Arc and Clare of Assisi. But I was never sure and never asked. I knew I could never choose Joan of Arc because Joan was very brave, and I was not. I knew with resignation that I would have to stay closer to the more domestic saints.

I would have to go with Saint Anne or Elizabeth, Jesus's relatives. Elizabeth was John the Baptist's mother. And Saint Anne, after twenty years of praying, was visited by an angel and given a child, Mary, who had the special assignment to become the mother of Jesus. God entered Mary through her ear. With a whisper, she conceived his son, Jesus. He must have been using the most luscious language with Mary— whispering and coaxing enough to conceive Jesus. I often thought of this and thought it only right that poetry would be God's vehicle—language as semen. It was right, very right.

I thought also that I should consider my nun name to be Elizabeth. Elizabeth, who waited diligently for eighty years to finally be visited by Gabriel the archangel and, through grace and power, conceive Saint John the Baptist, Jesus's cousin. I had this inclination to see everything as a bruise or a possible bruise and therefore felt someone like Saint Elizabeth could teach me to simply focus on fetching water and wait for the unexpected.

I knew for me it was the domestic. It was about finding the right shelf for the towels and good kitchen shelf paper. It was about understanding children and knowing when to kiss the bruised knee. If I could master towels and happiness, maybe salvation could be possible.

How is it, I wondered with guilt, that I could never get on top of the dishes or that I resented the children? They complained about my inadequate cooking (chicken casserole with canned cream of mushroom soup!). Why was my default look a glare when my children asked for something? It didn't matter what—I just resented that there was always a need. Why did I give in to my desire to snap at them when they complained about my inability to properly cut cheese or my knack for buying mismatched dishes? That is why, if I were to be a nun, I could never model myself after the more ambitious saints like Joan or Clare—Clare, with her warm caresses for the lepers.

As I was walking up the long sidewalk to the front door of the convent, I stared intently at that sidewalk. The color was called desert rose, Sister Joan had said. I wished I knew the name of the pink on the monastery walls. I wanted to name the color desert dove because the doves loved the gargoyles, and the color reminded me a little of sunset, but the name really evoked nothing of a visual nature, I conceded to myself.

There were two types of people who arrived at the convent the same time I did. People like me: searchers—the nuns called us "advisees." Sister Joan Clara was my spiritual adviser; she was to guide me through prayer. Then there were the homeless people. The nuns distributed daily bus passes to them—first come, first served—no questions asked. I was both jealous and nervous around my homeless compatriots. Jealous because I imagined a certain comfort in knowing so directly what your needs were. Yes, scared too. Would they hurt me? Would I be one of them? With my children? It had been six months since I lost my job.

I did not want to talk too directly about my homelessness concerns to Sister Joan Clara. I admit, though, that I loved watching the sister distribute the bus passes; she was compassionate and efficient all at the same time. "Good morning . . . next," she would say again and again till all the tickets were gone. Eventually, Sister Joan Clara and I would settle into a small room with many crucifixes and chairs from the 1970s. After a prayer, I would start. I would wring my hands on my lap. I wanted a lot.

I wanted mostly for my pain to stop. I wanted my money back from Frank. I wanted to know why I was so dumb. I wanted to know if my children would be OK. I wanted my husband to get better or go away. I wanted him to understand that his breakdowns, which required me to drive him to the hospital, were getting on my last nerve. I wanted him to get to the hospital himself when his delusions started. I wanted my kids to forgive me everything.

I wanted a handwritten letter from God. In the letter, I wanted an apology, a declaration of peace between the two of us. God should send a guarantee that my children's gene pool would be invisible to any mental illness searching for a home. I wanted God to admit to being inconsolable. That he felt the failure of providing free will and the pain and suffering it caused. That he lamented and suffered for humans failing each other and that he really had no excuses. That God, like me, had complicated the destiny of children. She had handed them questionable genes, my sadness, no money, intense love—and those were the raw materials of their future. It wasn't fair to them. I was not fair to my children. God had not been fair either.

"God *is* inconsolable," Sister Joan Clara tried to say in between the items on my list. It was the only thing on the list that Sister Joan Clara could guarantee. "I know God is inconsolable. I know that all the beads and crucifixes of the world cannot make up for the fact that we have used free will like a credit card for suffering. We have always done that and will continue to do so. God is inconsolable, yes. But the greater mystery might be why does God love?" Then I would cry and cry and cry.

Sister Joan Clara asked me if I wanted to discuss my brother Jim's death—not a random request, I knew. I had been very close to my brother, who had died four years ago. However, I was surprised how his death first came up. Sister Joan Clara had asked me, at our first meeting, how my "prayer life" was. I had to admit that since my brother's death, there had been no prayer life—sometimes, maybe, a prayer or two when I wanted to get my mind off of things.

Sister Joan Clara again reminded me that I had stopped talking to God ever since Jim's death.

"I miss him and think it is too hard sometimes to be without him."

"But, Joy, you have not cried enough. I can see that," the kind sister replied.

"But it is a black hole of grief," I said.

"God wants to hear all of your concerns, and God can be as big as any black hole if you need that, Joy."

"What is the use?" I wanted to know.

"The use is that you are not of use to yourself," she said.

"Sister, that is a little bit like a Zen koan. Can't you get in trouble with that? You know, for spiritual hopping?"

We laughed, and Sister said, "You don't know the half of it. We take from wherever there is God. Let's pray." And we did.

"I will try later tonight, Sister—to cry about Jim." With that, the session was over, and Sister Joan Clara shut the door behind me.

What I always noticed was that when she left the monastery, the homeless were gone. They had received their passes and had moved on.

Ted makes two appearances in this tale even though Joy doesn't know them

Homeless crackheads and nuns have some things in common. Notably, neither of us believe in asking why. Why is there suffering? Nuns know suffering is due to free will. Junkies suffer because of their need for a hit.

Crackheads like me know that we have given our free will over to the body. The body, in return, has given our lives away to drugs. For the junkie, there is no consultation between the body, heart or mind like there might be for the nuns. During my highs, I get to watch the disastrous things a junkie does for the body and its need. I have thrown myself in front of a car, stolen from my mom and hit a homeless dog just because he reminded me of me. The junkie's body believes in the next high, and everything is in service of that. For the junkie, there is no why, just when. When can the body get high again and forget that it exists? We junkies are so stupid because in our nonexistent mind, we think we can outsmart ourselves. That we can shoot up one more time and it won't hurt, not me, not anyone.

Nuns, like junkies, have come to the same conclusion about suffering, just by a different route. They know there is no use in understanding. They know that free will was God's greatest mess-up, and that makes them, these religious people, very busy. I guess if it weren't for junkies and other greed fiends, though, the nuns would have no job security. I love the nuns I hit up because they don't really care about me or about saving my soul, so they ask no questions. They don't want to hang out with me; they just want to be good to me and move on. It's like we poor people are the assembly lines for the religious. We provide steady and monotonous work. Why those nuns smile as they give me a little something, though, that surprises me. They smile and then shut the door on me.

My girlfriend is a junkie too, and we got separated. We went to a crack house—though it is hardly correct to say "crack house" because these houses are just as likely to have meth; meth is quicker and easier to find. But crack is still cheaper and a little easier to steal. Of course, we will take anything. I say this with no pride; it is simply a fact.

My girlfriend and I have figured out a few things. If we show up at the nuns' convent in the morning, we can get a free bus pass and ride the bus all day. If you're using meth, that can be extremely useful. Inside the bus, the temperature is regulated, unlike your body on meth, which can freeze or heat up in an arbitrary way. Also, you can get out and walk the aisles of stores and look; looking is all you need to do. Stealing is out of the question; you are so suspect because of your dirt and smell. Kate and I have the habit of riding the bus till around 11:00 a.m. That is about as soon as you can get drugs. For some reason, the dealers sleep in or have families they need to say goodbye to.

The day after I lost my girlfriend, I went to the convent. One of the sisters was on the patio watering, and she said, "God bless you. You do not look very well today." I told her how I had misplaced Kate. I don't really know why I felt a need to tell her that. She asked my name, and I told her. "Ted," she said, "can't you get some help for your addiction? We can't help you; you must seek the professionals. How did this happen to you?"

That was a good question and one I had not thought of, so I just said the words my mouth formed. "Sister," I said, "it was just there. The drugs were just there. I just took it. I just thought it would be like pot or something, but it wasn't."

"Have you ever gotten help?"

"Well, when the cops pick me up, I get to go into treatment. But after I get out, I am not sure what to do, and I see an old buddy or something. It is stupid or crazy."

I asked her why she wasn't afraid of us—I was not the only drug addict or homeless person who comes around. "Oh, the police keep a special watch on us. We have cameras and a hidden alarm we can use. We try to be sensible and charitable at the same time." I didn't know if I should laugh or cry. I never thought I would get much information from any straight person, much less a nun.

"Ted," she said, "I am worried about you and the way you look. You are bruised."

"Hey," I said, "I am just a junkie, and so is my old lady. We have gotten separated."

"Are you worried about her, Ted?"

I decided to be completely honest with her. "Yeah. One moment I am, and the next moment I am more worried about my fix."

She looked at me with aplomb; she did not fret over my statement. "Listen, Ted, I want you to know that you're loved and full of grief. You must find your girlfriend."

I did not have any idea what she meant. "Sister," I said, "how am I going to do that?"

"Ted, I have no idea, but I will pray." Then she said, "Ted, I am going to take the hose that I am holding, and I am going to place it on the crown of your head. I am going to rinse you a little. It is a simple and proper thing to do, and you will dry quickly in our desert town, and you will be refreshed. Jesus was baptized in the desert. Jesus loved water, you know."

I asked her if this was some sort of secret religious thing. She laughed and said, "No, unless you want it to be."

I got my bus pass, got soaked and then I left. I thought it would be good to look for my girlfriend. She might have drugs for me, and if not, that would be all right. I had an idea. I would find clean and cool water for Kate like I had just had. It felt good. I would bathe her a little; maybe it would just be around her neck, and that would be OK too.

Let's hear from Frank

Many of the things that have happened I have not wanted to happen. As I told Joy, I am crazy. "How crazy are you?" she asked. I told her I was crazy enough to qualify for four hours of therapy on Tuesday and Thursdays. This was a subtlety that was lost on her, I think—which is fine because I have no idea how my state "psychiatric team" came up with this anyway. I am a client of the state. That is how clearly and finally Joy has given up on me. I used to be so angry about it, but actually things have worked out pretty well for me.

I hate it when Joy doesn't answer her phone. I know she knows it's me, and I know when she is trying to ignore me. That's what happened on the night her brother chased me around the block, grabbed me and held me until the police came. That is how I ended up for two weeks in the dungeon of the state mental institution. Believe me, this is very different from the private hospital I was in just a short month before. In the private crazy place, Desert Respite for the Mentally Ill, there was time and attention—group therapy three times a day, a daily psychiatric visit. I also had a very beautiful Serbian psychiatrist, though she had an awful hair-dye job, reddish/orange. She told me something that I think I knew and maybe even Joy knows—that I am probably a genius, but the problem is I have narcissistic personality disorder. That was why, she explained, I was so sensitive and easily hurt.

This helped me understand myself quite a bit—helped me know that Joy was probably right when she said I cared for my fear above all things. But she should have added that I had my fear because of my incredible ability to see things at their bone. I knew that someone interviewing me for a job was only trying to feel validated in his or her own universe and with colleagues. It wasn't genuine at the core. It caused many hardships, I know. And someone can play the game—you know, be excellent at a job or with people even if it meant not acknowledging your own intelligences and gifts. I couldn't. Call it real or call it a copout—it was what I did, for better or worse.

There were some people I felt comfortable with: "outsiders." This is why I am so good at ethnic cooking, secondhand stores, and why I bonded with the one-armed driving instructor who was so useful in helping me get my driver's license at age thirty-eight. We got along well, I thought, and I was surprised when Joy decided to join us on our lessons. I am sure it was her idea—her sense of a good time.

The doctor at Desert Respite changed my dosage; she felt a need to decrease the antipsychotic.

This was done because of my intelligence. She wanted me to have more access to that. I can't regret what happened because of that hospitalization and the aftereffects. By reducing the antipsychotics, I had profound access to everything. I went to see Mose Allison, and the music, the notes; I could feel them on my bones and in my blood—extraordinary and horrible at the same time and incredible.

That night of the concert, I stayed up all night. I was able to talk, talk, I tell you, to the Highest of Powers. As I write this, even with some distance, I can remember the walking and singing down the alley behind my house. I smoked a few cigarettes and noticed, actually loved, the falling and lingering of smoke in my lungs. I came to understand God, Joy, and even violence for love. I came to understand why one would want to burn. That night, I was able to mathematically identify what God is. I am going to share that with you. The formula for God is: $1 = TH/xNg = w+chil\%Bastrd/frek$. Don't bother putting this into a computer. It will not work, and you will feel entitled to say whatever you want about me. But if you see the complexity and the nuance of this, that God is literally music and math, you can see so many other things. You can take Joy's name and filter it through this formula. Please don't make me explain. I don't have time. You can filter Joy's name and see so clearly it means "go on." Go on and destroy, weep, and happiness is in the weeping.

I tried to call Joy to tell her this. No answer. No answer. No answer. I did, however, notice that Joy had left a message. When I retrieved it, it was her tiny voice. That voice makes me so sad. She said that she lost her job that very day.

Excellent, I thought. She can help me do God's work. She can pick up the sword with me. When she didn't answer, again, I knew where she was: her sister's house. I ran there, with excitement and need. We had so much work to do. I ran to the house. I pounded on the door—I didn't have time for the doorbell; they are so bourgeois anyway. I pounded; I could see through the window next to the door that Joy was coming; she was going to answer the door. But her sister— she is so evil—pulled her back.

So I ran to the neighbor's house—I knew her slightly. I began to shout the God news and pound on her door. That I had the power to understand the meaning of names. I knew that Joy and I were warriors and needed to take up swords. I said all those things and was happy and determined.

Suddenly, Joy's brother was there, Michael. I ran, he chased me, the police came.

The thing about the state hospital where Michael told the police and ambulance to take me as opposed to the private hospital is the light. At the state hospital, the quality of light is gray. Also, I seldom saw a doctor, no therapy. Once there was therapy, art therapy, and I wrote and illustrated a poem for Joy. In this piece of art, I talked about Joy as a cunt, how she had destroyed my life and wasted my time when I had so much work to do—she had destroyed me by putting me in this godforsaken place.

She had destroyed me by choosing her sister and brother over me the night I was taken to the hospital. Even the children came first for her, always. How can that be? Any marriage counselor will tell you that you must put the marriage first. My marriage is to myself now. Two weeks in the state hospital. God, how I hate Joy's family.

I can see and know that I was psychotic, but it doesn't mean I wasn't happy and deeply touched by everything—I felt infused. I am in a halfway house now, ward of the state and all. I have carved a location for myself here among the crazy people. I am the cook just like I was for Joy, her sister and brother—they loved my cooking, and they should; it was good.

I have a girlfriend too. Linda is younger than I am, and that means we mostly watch movies. We met in a doctor's waiting room. I noticed her skin right away. It was clear and white. Though she has troubles of her own, she does not have the furrowed forehead that was implanted on Joy. She is not a reader. And why should she be? She is part of the postliterate culture, where the visual reigns. We are not picky about what we watch, whatever is available at the public library, seasons one and three of the *Gilmore Girls*. I introduced her to that one because I watched it with Tess, about the fast-talking and ironic mother-daughter team that reigned supreme is some small-town village in Connecticut or something like that.

Joy and I used to read poetry together. Our favorite poet was Walt Whitman. We loved especially "The Wound-Dresser": "What stays with you latest and deepest? of curious panics. Of hard-fought engagements or sieges tremendous what deepest remains?"

How careful Joy and I wanted to be with each other's wounds. The way Walt Whitman was with the Civil War soldiers'. We wanted to be that careful and gentle. I can say it now: We failed. We failed completely.

Joy visits Frank
in the south side psychiatric
hospital and Jake at the
east side rehab center

I needed to be careful. I had lost my job. My husband was
in the psychiatric hospital on the south side. My son was
in drug rehabilitation on the east side. I wanted to save gas.
That is what I thought about. Is there a way to conserve gas
because I cannot be wasteful, and I have lost my job, and my
husband is in a psychiatric hospital and my son is in drug
rehabilitation. In the evenings, I was proud of this thought
in a mild way. I did not have dire thoughts—about death or
leaving my children—rather, how to be economical.

I decided it would be useful, in the saving-gas department, if I did not run the air conditioner. I remembered my
brother Jim and my father discussing once whether or not it
saved gas. Jim was taking an auto-repair class for one college
credit, and he had learned it didn't matter. My father argued
otherwise: "It only makes sense. There is stuff going on in
the engine, and the engine requires gas. So it has to pull the
gasoline in."

"Engines don't work that way," Jim claimed. But, in truth, neither was really sure of the facts of his argument. They were idea people, and engines, well, an engine was a fact.

I did not remember the conclusion of the conversation. But that it happened, that I remembered that it happened seemed significant to me. It was the desert and warm, so when I drove and cried, the windows would steam up on the inside. "Did it use gas to turn on the windshield wipers? Oh, wait, windshield wipers were for the outside. The crying and fogged windows were on the inside." It was like that inside my mind. A little like slow motion or a bad-dubbing job, where the words and the logic were just slightly off.

I decided I needed to roll down the window to cry. I had to organize my crying. So I cried before I left the house to see Frank. And if I needed to, I could pull over—once—and cry underneath a palm tree on the way to the hospital, but that was awfully close to a main street so not ideal. There was a bank of eucalyptus trees, twenty of them between Frank's hospital and Jake's rehab. They were on a street I knew that was quiet and a little hidden. They were across from the park where Jake played soccer as a kid, before drugs. Sometimes I would get out and walk and stop and cry at every fifth tree. But once I found myself smiling. "I have gone from soccer mom to a rehab mom."

On a bad day, I would walk the bank of eucalyptus trees and touch each one, their smooth, clean bark. On one particularly bad day, I realized I had never asked myself, "Could I have done something different?" Yes, of course, I could have done something different. It was just that it eluded me. Crying under the eucalyptus trees, I thought I should have had Jake on a different team so he could have made friends in the neighborhood. Maybe I could have spent more time practicing kicking with him? But time, where could that have come from? I remembered once saying to my sister, "Maybe I don't do enough?"

This surprised Debra. "Really?" she asked. "How would that work?"

This nostalgia for what may have been had always been a form of bad taste to me. It was an activity for a people I did not belong to. Those who made normal bad decisions—a wrong car purchase, even a wrong spouse. A mistake that was painful and time-consuming but a mistake that was made on solid ground. My mistakes were not like that. On the day I was driving to the psychiatric hospital to tell Frank we must divorce, I thought of the professor I had had an affair with and gotten pregnant. "What was his name?" I could not remember. "Oh, yes, Mark. I wonder if he is dead?" I tried to make a note to look him up on the internet. Why have this thought now? I remembered reading that time/space break down when a mind is in crisis. Is that what is happening, that my placement markers were gone, and I could suddenly care about someone I actually never cared about? Then this thought: how sad to have a profound history with someone who occupied so little of me. Is this what it is like to lose your mind? Is this the side effect of my crises to have a non sequitur like Mark intrude? But where was he? Did he have children? I wondered without malice but as a visitor to a foreign planet. I was my own foreign planet.

Though I had forgotten Mark, the abortion never escaped me. I still visited a priest at least once a year and confessed the abortion, as if it had just happened. I remembered the first time I did this, and the priest said, "The problem with abortion is I have never met anyone who could forgive themselves. Your penance is to find a way to forgive yourself."

"Like how?" I asked.

"The Ten Commandments?" he said it as if it were a question.

One priest said, "Do something life-affirming." I pinpoint my profound desire to have children to that conversation. Another said to pray daily. But I always did that, I thought, and then remembered that worry was different from prayer.

None of it ever worked, completely. I did think about the abortion more than I thought I would.

And that was a punishment and sorrow. How ancient that grief now was. My thoughts during those times were not maudlin, full of what-ifs, but, rather, was that the beginning of losing my body? I could not decide. The children provided solidness, an anchor, but then how fluid I had become as they got older. It was sad to me, my fluidity; it meant that I was not solid, that I had given that up. In my efforts to expand myself for my children, I became less solid, more ethereal. At some point, I became unable to answer the simplest question. "Why can't I decorate the kite with tin cans and have it float at the same time?" I remembered Jake asking, and I could not explain. I did not know.

Out of love for my children and Frank, I had dispersed myself, my knowledge, my skills, and my very precarious abilities to negotiate the world. Frank, it turns out, had even fewer than I did. I remembered wanting to marry Frank because when he said he loved me, I believed him. Solid people would have asked, "Can you be my partner? Can you work with me?" That never occurred to me. That was a side effect of the abortion; I believed that. The forgetting to ask questions and to imagine well into the future.

I spent each day traveling to visit Frank on the south side and Jake on the east side. I was pleased that I planned a route that allowed me to save gas and to cry. The day I determined to tell Frank that we needed to divorce was like any of the days I visited. I always arrived at the psychiatric hospital after arts and crafts. I was not sure if this was because they were always having arts and crafts or if it was more serendipitous. Frank was in the locked part of the hospital. This was because of the way he landed in the hospital. On the day I lost my job, I sat stupefied with the children on my sister Debra's couch. Frank, meanwhile, was down the street talking to God. He could not find me to tell me the good news: that he and I needed to take up swords for the battle. Later, he would tell me that he did not mean real swords and that he was very disappointed in me that I did not understand his figurative language. My sister, Debra, would not let him in. He started to go to the neighbor's house, and that was when my brother arrived and began the chase that landed Frank against his will in the county psychiatric hospital.

My obligations to Frank were now completely unmanageable. Why I felt so obligated was, finally, beginning to dawn on me during those dark and eventful days. Not until those moments, not even briefly, did I question that assumption. Once again, maybe these obligations were rooted in losing my body, the chaffing away over the years; my attempts to be more had worn me away, a rock pounded by the sea. I never gave Frank up. It would have been a good idea, but I did not because the body that I had, that would have required this action, did not exist; it was depleted, gone.

The hospital had several layers of security. Three doors before I was buzzed into Frank's area. Those who buzzed me in were professionals or bored, I could not tell. They looked beyond me. Not curious about me at all. I hated that moment of anonymity and wished for more scrutiny—an accusatory look perhaps. It might have helped me understand how real this place was. Instead, I was treated as if invisible. Perhaps this was their way of being kind? By pretending we poor souls do not exist?

On a previous visit, when Frank saw I was buzzed in, he shouted out across the community room, "Joy, today we had arts and crafts, and I wrote a book. It is called *My Wife Is a Cunt.*" What I feared was that this comment would get Frank in lockdown. No one paid any attention. I wondered if I was getting my jail movies confused with my mental-hospital movies. Frank's comment caught no one's attention. Not the nurse enclosed in the nurse's station, not Frank's psychiatric colleagues—they seemed to be watching car racing on the television.

Frank said, "Let me read my book to you. It is an oversize book."

"Yes, it is indeed," I replied. Frank had used eighteen-by-twenty-four-inch paper, folded down the middle and stapled. But I pleaded, "Could you read it a little quieter so we don't disturb people?" I nodded my head toward the couch, trying to indicate "people," but I am not sure what was actually communicated.

"OK," Frank said in a stage whisper. "As I said, it is called

My Wife Is a Cunt." That was written on the title page. The first page had floating beds and screwdrivers on it. The second page said, "My wife is a double-decker cunt." The third page was a zebra page, lots of black and white lines. The fourth page said, "The End."

It was the words "The End" that got to me. Had me recalling our beginnings in Seattle. Our walks. How Frank served me warm soups. How I once got soaked in the rain, and he drew a warm bath.

"Thank you, Frank," I said, thinking of the bath.

He said, "Well, you are welcome. I would let you have the book, but I kind of like it myself."

"It's OK," I replied. "I understand. Hey, Frank," I asked, "can you tell me about some of your colleagues here?"

Frank began and then stopped. "I don't know. War victims, I think. My roommate is a war victim, and he shouts and paces, so they overmedicate him. I don't really talk to him or anyone."

"Why not?" I asked.

Frank said, "I am not that type of crazy."

"What kind of crazy are you?" I asked. "What kind?"

"I am the kind of crazy that knows too much. Someone who can see the formula for God. All I need is someone to follow me and keep up with my thoughts. You won't do that, will you, Joy? That is the type of crazy that I am."

"I guess I miss the type of crazy when you could cook and drive and pretty much mess things up. But, you know, you were still around. Kind of. You know? The old crazy—that was what I was nostalgic for, Frank."

"Oh, I am way beyond that," said Frank.

"When did it happen?" I wondered and suddenly appreciated that Frank never really blamed his insanity on me. If he were cruel, he could have done that.

Instead, Frank had different theories about his insanity. He told me one of them on that visit: "I am way beyond the old insanity. I have seen too much. Sometimes I want to sue, sue somebody, but I am not sure whom, maybe the makers of standardized tests. Those who have whipped us away from our own selves by forcing us to ask how things work and not why. Why do they work? This life, our life? And why doesn't it work because, Joy, it is both. You and I—it has been both. That is all I want to know. Sometimes I take the medicine they give me and it works. The racing is gone. Other times, the racing stays. Shouldn't medicine work always? No, because each time I take medicine, a different mind is taking it. Still my mind but different."

It was getting confusing for me. So what I said next was this: "We will need to divorce. Because I have no money. Because I cannot carry you anymore. Because I was never what you needed. Because time is of the essence here. I will need to serve you these papers while you are here in the psychiatric hospital. Thank you, Frank."

Frank said, "Why do you keep saying 'thank you'? Joy, look where you have put me. This place has no windows." I noticed for the first time that although we were in the desert and the days were reaching a pitched brightness, this psychiatric hospital lacked light and color. That you needed to crane your neck to see outside the small windows that were several feet above the floor.

"That must be sad, Frank; you like light," I said.

"Yes, I like light, Joy. It was why I was able to move to

this fucking desert town, because there was a sky. I didn't have that when I was growing up. I had water. Gray water and a gray sky. Now I have no light. It is what troubles me the most. I should be worried about you and the kids, is that what you're thinking? Well, the kids are the same as light. You, fucking Joy, have put me here, and you are only gray water." Frank laughed. "I don't care if we divorce. I don't care if I belong to the state now. It is better for me, for us. Joy, send in the papers."

I got up and said, "Thank you." The papers, in fact, were already drawn.

I called the legal courier on my way to the eucalyptus trees. The eucalyptus trees, "always after Frank but before Jake," I said to remind and orient myself. Arrangements were made to have the papers delivered to Frank at the psychiatric hospital. That was how my marriage ended: Frank in a psychiatric hospital, Jake in drug withdrawal, and me jobless.

On my way to see Jake, I thought about my son and could not help but be impressed, moved by Jake's determination to get over his craving for drugs. He had always been like that, determined. A determination to make dinosaur sculptures, determination to ride a bike, determination to create cities from every shoe in the house. His drug withdrawal reminded me of how fussy and colicky he was as a newborn. There was no position he could tolerate for long. Nothing I could do to soothe him. He was angry, too, it seemed to me, already so angry. As an infant, he was able to vomit and piss on me at the same time.

These seventeen years later, it was the same. He would pace his room, smoke cigarettes. Once he pushed me against the wall and, with a mad look, demanded that I make it better. Then he wept in an otherworldly way. I held on to the doorknob as he demanded and then melted to the ground. I left then. My son on the floor. I did not know any of Jake's friends in his rehab program. It was different there. This was not school, where I needed to be nice to other kids, hoping they would return the favor to Jake. Nor did I have to make nice with the other rehab parents. What a relief. They were as stunned as I was. In addition, they were nice, maybe even nicer than I was. That was one of the first things the counselor said: "Nice has nothing to do with addiction. You are all nice, and your kids are too. Probably too nice. They didn't want to reject their friends. And you—meaning all of us—didn't want to be the heavy. You put the pause button on your suspicions. You hesitated before you said no. Parents, it is time to take the pause off no."

I was guilty. I knew that. I was either too intrigued by Jake's lies or too scared of what was behind them. We had a rule when the kids were young that they could not get in trouble if they told the truth.

That was my way of avoiding what I knew—which is they, we, are all liars. I, who told each of my children never to lie, could not be straight with anyone. The nice thing about being a rehab mom is you could admit to this. It was necessary. How far back did my lying go? Forever, pretending I knew how to fix his upset stomach, or that I was not tired, that I didn't mind his beautiful and colicky body. That he didn't hurt me.

Then there were the lies about how I didn't mind that he was intense, demanding, unusual, a curious presence in the world that I insisted on renaming "interesting." How easy it was to call his drug use adolescence. Reckless. A continuation of his intense demand as a child. All by way of saying I had no idea how to manage my brilliant stranger, my son. I directed us, Jake and me, to what we had in common, for the possible and imaginary, all the while excusing that neither one of us had an ability to be here on earth and to see and say that it was a problem.

The same evening I told Frank about the divorce, I went to the parent support group with my sister, Debra. It was a bit of a gift, I knew, to be able to enter into this world of drug rehab with someone, a companion. They were a motley crew. Grandparents, single moms and dads, all sorts of economic situations. I was a bit taken aback by the angry ones and was envious of them, their outrage and their sense of betrayal. I wished that I could feel betrayed by Jake, but I did not. Rather, in this place, I felt that I was watching a movie in a language I did not understand. Concepts from the counselors and the other parents would float by, and I would try to latch on to them. "Just say no" was one. "Develop a support system" was another. I thought of my sister, Debra, sitting next to me—"support" and "system." I kept seeing them as two words that needed to come together.

"Like Debra," I said to myself, trying to learn a new concept while relying wholly on it.

Debra was abrupt. She interrupted her compatriots, only to admonish them to ask for help from their no-good husband/son/daughter/brother/sister. She had a historical fact for every tale. "Buzz Aldrin has walked on the moon, and he struggled with addiction." She wanted her cohorts to know and to be encouraged. Laura, whose son was court-ordered—graffiti and pot—wanted to know who Buzz Aldrin was. "Remember the moon?" Debra said. "One step for mankind, et cetera? Well, Buzz Aldrin was with the guy who said that."

"But why do I care if Buzz has addiction problems?"

"I am just saying," Debra said, "if someone can go to the moon and confront his addictions, so can . . . "

"I just want my son to make curfew," said Laura.

There were two populations of kids there: those who were there due to the courts and kids like Jake, who wanted to come. I received a call from the hospital two days after I lost my job. An overdose of some unknown substance. When I walked in, he said, "Mom, I need some help." Would I ever forgive myself for thinking, "Can I afford a drug addict?" and not "By any means necessary"? Debra stepped up for that assignment. She found the place, walked with me to fill out the paperwork, found a way to have it paid for.

"It has an excellent reputation," Debra said, as if she had just found a good deal on an exotic resort. "Very little relapsing. And here they drug-test the kids, so they know they can't use."

"Thank you, Debra," I said, sounding out each syllable.

In group therapy, Debra was telling one of the parents to expect more from her sister. I wondered how much Debra told this parent about us. I hoped Debra had not said too much about Frank's odd behaviors and how I worry about the kids in relation to Frank. Our brother had been dead two years, and he was my confidant. So what had evolved with Debra was new during this disaster.

Debra enjoyed her role as a problem solver; she had started to give me lists of things to do. At first, I could not even make out the letters, but I got better and even did the items on the list: "Make a phone call, cook dinner, and pay one bill." I began to depend on the lists. But who was this Debra sitting next to me? What sorrows did she hold with her arms folded across her chest unless she was rapidly pointing to someone? I did not know, and when I asked, Debra laughed. "Let's make that question 'What happiness does Debra have?'"

Jake and the other kids at some point would join us and sit with their respective families. And the parents would fall in love with someone else's kid. I loved Sal, from Saudi Arabia. He drank a six-pack of beer and passed out while trying to get on his bicycle. Sal thought it was unfair. He knew someone who got drunk and drove his car into a neighbor's garage but got off because of an illegal search. I loved how athletic he seemed and that his anger was adolescent—overly concerned with what was fair and equal. Jake had given up a long time ago, hoping that things would shake up in some even way. None of my children had ever wondered about what was fair. That would have been a luxury, to wonder why things shook out the way they did. We were only ever interested, especially these past few months, in if it was possible to find shelter, a very simple but complete bomb shelter.

The day I told Frank we were going to divorce, I had to go into the "fishbowl" with Jake. That meant we sat in the middle of a circle, surrounded by the other families. In this exercise, we each needed to say what we resented and what we missed. Jake resented my absent-mindedness, my forgetting the most basic things—to cook dinner. He missed me not being sad. He could barely remember a time I wasn't sad. I missed Jake as a constant sketcher, always creating and sketching. I resented his drug withdrawals and that he wanted me there to witness how terrible they were. I thought it was an added punishment. I felt bad about that, too, I confessed. I wanted to be strong enough for Jake and his withdrawals; I wanted to be that good. Then we hugged each other, awkwardly but with a confidence that Jake was done with drugs. The counselor explained that Jake, I, and Debra were lucky that Jake crashed and burned so quickly—he had used drugs for only nine months. That Jake was able to see early on that he would die if he continued to use was good news.

After family therapy, I would gather the girls up from my brother Michael's house. They were cleaned and homework done. I would have them crawl into my bed and listen to warm and sad Celtic music. They would do the things that used to make them happy—make up words, rhyme their names. Once, Mia remembered how they would write on each other's back in an invisible language. Mia wanted her back written on again in invisible language. "OK," I said and began to write on Mia's back.

Mia said, "What is the invisible language saying?"

And I said, still writing, "This invisible language is telling you, Mia and Tess, about the invisible bridge to spring. You get there by going under a mountain of leaves and giving Father Winter a bribe. You must trick him, Mia and Tess, and this will be hard to do because he loves the cold, but you must trick him into believing it is spring. You do this with the wind." I blew gently on Mia's back. "And if the wind keeps up, it will blow the snow away, and Father Snow will think it is time to go away, and that is what he will do. He will go away. And what is the best thing about spring?" I asked. "It is that spring is empty by itself. It needs you to love it and to see how magnificent the flowers and smells are. Mia, can you make spring beautiful this year?"

Mia said, "I don't have to answer that because it was written in an invisible language."

"Well, write the answer on my back and tell me what you are writing in the invisible language. Like I did."

"I don't want to," said Mia, and she began to cry. Then Tess began to cry.

I swooped them, one in each arm. I held Mia and said, "Of course you don't. Not now. You can make it spring tomorrow."

After Mia quieted, I asked Mia and Tess what the best thing was about their day. Mia said it was that she was named producer of the class play. "What does that mean?" I asked.

"It means I get to decide what the props are, where they go."

"Tess, what about you?"

"Sam, who has said some pretty crude things about my appearances, did not speak to me today. That was the best thing."

"Ah," Mia and I said together, but it was Mia who asked, "Can't you do better than that, Tess?" Tess scowled at her and was about to begin one of her litanies about how life was hard for her, easy for Mia, and she, Mia, better start understanding that. Mia and I both put up our hands to signal that Tess could stop—we got it.

Tess asked me about how my day was, and I thought hard and carefully. *This could matter*, I thought to myself. "I saw your father and told him we were going to have to reorganize the family again. This time, we will still love him, but we will divorce. In the long term, it will be best."

Mia appeared to be thinking about this, and she said, "My friend Haley says that it looks like you are divorced anyway because you don't really live together. At first, I wanted to argue with her, but then I just shrugged my shoulders."

"Well, it doesn't matter what we call it, only that we love and take care of each other," I offered. Mia snuggled against me. "You know what else was great about my day?" I said. And to their quizzical looks, I said, "I did not use the air conditioner in the car when I drove. That means I might have saved two cents in gasoline. If I keep this up, we will be millionaires before you know it." They both shook their heads in disbelief. There was their mom again, not making sense, being on the verge of silly.

Mia said, "Mom, it would be nice to have a girl bed, where we all sleep together, but I really hate it when you start screaming in your sleep, when you start saying, 'No, no, no.' Is there any way you could not do that?"

"Mia," I said, "I am feeling good about the night. I believe I am not going to scream once. Unless it is to say, 'Mia is magnificent. Tess is terrific.' If I yell that, can you work with it?"

Mia rolled her eyes and said, "Write on my back again in invisible ink." I did. I wrote, "I love you, Mia!"

On that night, I did not wake up screaming. Not even once.

Mia has a scary dream but does not want to wake her mother

I did sleep with my mom on and off till I was eleven. I am twelve now.

I would wake up in the middle of the night, and it would be dark. I would wake up and think about it. How I was scared and wondered if there was someone in the closet, even though I knew I was just seeing the dark bulk of my mother's winter coat that hung in my room for some reason that never made sense to me. She would say, "It is safer there." I never understood that.

On the other hand, I didn't think about whether or not I would go to my mother's room. I just automatically went. She didn't seem to mind. She would just move over. If she was sound asleep, she would place the palm of her hand in between my shoulder blades. If she was awake even a little, she would tickle my back. It was like having my very own protection machine.

What is great is that my mom, when she is awake, can be annoying because she is always distracted. During these night moments, I was not competing with anyone. I have heard my aunt use the word *essence*; she says it is a person's truest self. My mom automatically putting her palm between my shoulder blades or tickling me, I think that is her truest self, and I like that.

It would be more accurate to say my "parents' room" because for a while our dad was still with us. In those days, I would sleep with my head at the bottom of the bed. It was later I moved closer to my mom. What I remember about my father is heaviness. The heaviness was a smell—a little like salad dressing that has gone bad. I did not like it, and it was scary too. In those days, when I would be at the bottom of the bed, my mom would hold my ankles, and just that would fix me from my fear—of the night and the smell.

I wish I felt different about my father. Something different from sadness and, I hate to say it, disgust. I don't have the memories, I suppose, even though my mom wants me to. I feel like he is a distant relative that I am supposed to be kind to.

My brother and sister teased me about sleeping with my mom, but they had no right to because they did their own share of sleeping in my parents' room. Anyway, ever since I was in sixth grade, I have determined to sleep on my own so that when I tell people I have my own room, I could mean it in all its aspects.

I just quit going in there. It was not easy. I did it in several stages. The first stage was having my mom put me to bed in my room at bedtime. I would ask her to tickle my back, and I tried to be a bit bratty as a way of letting her know I was not afraid and not small.

The next step was to make sure a nightlight was on. The closet light did not work for me because it made shadows that moved. The nightlight worked about half of the time—meaning I sometimes still ventured into my mother's room. This, however, was becoming unsatisfactory because I was beginning to enjoy having a whole bed to myself. Also, since my mom had lost her job and my father was committed to the psychiatric hospital, my mom started to scream in her sleep. Nothing too weird, just "no, no, no."

Given this new situation, I really wanted to sleep alone, even when one night I had a most terrible dream. It happened after my mother took me to see *The Wizard of Oz* downtown on the big screen. Maybe I went to bed too soon after we got home. In the dream, my father was a cross between himself and one of the monkeys. He was flying but wanted to land. I was standing below in a large corral, trying to guide him, waving my hands and saying, "Over here." Then I would say, "Now over there." Finally, it seemed like he was going to land, and so I ran to what looked like the right place. But he landed on the barbed-wire fence, and when I finally reached him, he wasn't there, just a cloud of dust or something.

The color of the earth and sky was so scary in the dream, a dark gray with pinks shooting through. I woke up with my heart pounding—but determined not to go into my mother's room. I noticed that there was a light on in the dining room. I followed it out and discovered Jake sitting at the table, smoking a cigarette.

"Put that cigarette out," I said. He acted startled and then put the cigarette out. I can be a little bossy with Jake because I don't think he has much common sense. "What are you doing here, Jake?" I asked.

"I am trying to figure out the lyrics to this Depeche Mode song, 'Personal Jesus.' Do you want to read me the lyrics?"

"Sure," I said and then read the lyrics out loud to him. The lyrics were about trusting faith and trusting when forgiveness is given. "Jake," I asked, "why this song at this time?"

"Do you promise not to tell Joy?"

"OK."

"I think I am in love."

"Whoa," I said. "Two things. Have you discussed this with your Alcoholics Anonymous sponsor, and what does this song have to do with being in love?"

He was exasperated with me, but I think he wanted to talk. Given the time, around midnight, he might have felt protected that our mom was not going to hear. "Yes, I have discussed it with my sponsor. My girlfriend, Rose, was never involved with my drugging, and so my sponsor is going to give it thumbs-up for now. We met in art class a couple years ago. But we just started talking a couple months ago. We are going slow because of my problems. I understand that I have made many people wary of me. Even you, Mia.

"This song, 'Personal Jesus,' it came on the radio while we were out the other night. It was on a channel I never listen to, but here was one of my favorite bands and singing a great song. Rose suggested that this could be our song. It made sense given it is about trust, faith and forgiveness."

I didn't know what to say after this. He was right; I am wary of him. This is quite different from what we used to be. I missed the small things. When he was using drugs, he quit wrestling with me and talking about the different genres of punk music. But my favorite thing was watching on the internet this great cartoon, *Daria*. Daria was this really smart teenage girl; she was so sarcastic and dismissive of the whole high-school scene—not just cheerleading but drugs and the need to be cool. Jake and I had to pull our chairs really close together and kind of leaned over the small screen. It was great, like being in a private universe. We never spoke but gestured—a random thumbs-up for a good line or a sideways glance to communicate some minor chore: adjust the volume or get a blanket to throw over our knees. When there were no more in the series, the screen showed up with large letters, something like "This show no longer available." We both stared straight ahead. Jake said, "What does it say?" I told him, and he just started crying. And I started crying.

Then he asked, "Why are we crying?"

And I said, "Because it is over, and it was really good." After that, we cried about five minutes longer. Then Jake got up and went into his room. We never talked about the show or our reaction ever again.

After Jake told me about his girlfriend, I decided to tell him about the dream. How the scariest part was waving my hands, trying to direct our dad and not knowing where he was going to land, and then he falls onto the darn barbed-wire fence.

When I was done, he said, "Damn, barbed wire, screws you every time." We both laughed at that. I told him I was scared, and I didn't want to go into mom's room. There was another long silence. Finally, he said, "Hey, do you want me to sit in your room with you?"

"Would you? Would you mind?"

"No."

He came into my room and sat on a chair. But that did

not feel quite right. So I said, "Would you mind tickling my back?" He agreed. He tried to be soothing while tickling over my nightgown. It felt terrible, nothing like my mother's touch. But I did use that as an opportunity to say, "Jake, I am glad you are OK."

"Mia," he said, "I am sorry I have not been a stellar brother. I want to change that for you."

"OK, then soften your touch there. That would be stellar." We both laughed. It didn't help. His tickling was not what I knew. Nothing like my mom's soft fingertips and the way she can make gentle circles with them. His fingernails were tough, and he seemed to just tickle one spot over and over again. Frankly, it was terrible. I pretended I was asleep. I didn't want to tell him to stop because I knew he was trying so hard. When he thought I was asleep, he leaned over and kissed my forehead and left. After he left, I clenched my fists and did some singing to myself, but I did not get up. Eventually, I fell asleep.

In the morning, my mom came in. She leaned over me and kissed me and said, "I am so proud you are getting to be independent, and I miss you."

"OK," I said, "but leave."

She replied, "OK, but you are not allowed to be rude," and she gave me the look. I have no idea what she means by *rude*. I try not to be rude, but she lingers and asks the stupidest questions. Whoever decided that parents get to ask at any time of the day or night, "How was school, and have you done your homework?"

I am more grown up and sophisticated than that. Of course I do my homework. But I am also a researcher and lover of John Lennon and middle-era Beatles music. Not that I want to discuss this with my mom, but I want her to provide me the time and opportunity to think through the lyrics. I mean, what is a "glass onion"? That can be difficult if you are going to believe there was more than drug-induced lyrics, like I do, although some of Jake's friends do not, I bet. The other thing I wonder about is why the *White Album* has so many references to guns and violence—is it predicting the future? I could come up with theories here, if only there were time and quiet in this family.

It is the interruptions that annoy me—mostly from my mom but Tess too. I could be very busy handwriting the lyrics of a song down because that is the best way to help me understand, but Tess will barge in to ask if she looks OK. "Yes," I will say. Then she will get really mad at me for not really looking.

If I tell my mom and Tess that I want to be alone, they look worried and rejected. They might send Jake to see if I am OK. Sometimes I can see my mom struggle like she knows she gets in the way. I know she has very little experience with someone like me, someone who prefers being alone. Jake needed so much attention with the dyslexia, and Tess . . . Tess just demands so much.

When my mom gives me that look, it is full of fear, as if she is afraid of losing me, but it is odd—is she scared I will run away? Is she scared that I have more secrets about my father, and she does not want to bear that possibility for me or for her? Once I actually said, "Quit looking at me like I am on the verge of running away! I am not interested in running away. I am not that desperate." She gave me a sad and puzzled look, which is equally annoying.

I like it when I can visit my aunt's house. She leaves me

alone, and if I ever get around to saying anything, she's going to think it is: (1) funny, (2) clever, or (3) very smart. Then she will make me repeat it in front of her husband, and that is about it. When I am around her house, I can expect close to four hours of silence.

My mom asked me to write a letter to Jake so they could discuss it in rehab. I tried to protest because I was embarrassed by the smallness of my issues. My mom said there was no such thing and encouraged me, so I did write that I missed wrestling and pretend fights and watching good shows with him. I told him I never quit loving him and never would. He later told me how important the letter was to him and hoped that we could get things back together and he could be my role model.

I mean no disrespect to Tess, but I think I have more sense than she does. She has been pretty angry with my dad, and she talks about it so much. How he said crazy things in front of her friends. How he let her down.

I suggested that she prioritize what she worries about. I told her how I decided that I could be concerned about Jake and my grades, and that is all. I cannot take on worrying and being upset with my father. Tess gets angry often about my father and about the same things. So when she freaks out about him—how he talked crazy in front of her friends or embarrassed her—I just shrug my shoulders or suck my cheeks in. I mean, what good is it going to do? This annoys Tess to no end, and once she even challenged me to a duel about it, but that made me laugh, and then she got really furious and threw herself on me and started hitting me. That made me laugh even more.

My mom still talks about that day as one of the weirder ones. "A duel?" she says. "Fist fighting between my girls? Mia laughing demonically? Is this a sign of the apocalypse?" Then Tess will get mad that my mom is using big words, and the whole thing gets on the verge of starting again.

My sadness about my father is like my mother's palm on my back, steady, constant. That is what Tess doesn't understand with all her hope that our family could be regained. But it can't be, so why bother with it? My father walking down the street with a determination, a knowledge of where he is going, those days are gone. Those great grilled-cheese sandwiches he would make, they are gone.

Sometimes I want to scream at Tess. It is like she has no understanding about grown-up things like disappointment and loss. I want to tell her she can have memories, but she cannot have hope. I want to scream, "Tess, give up the hope, please, give it up!" But I don't scream that. I just go into my room and read. Sometimes I do something to show her how smart I am. I don't know why, especially when I know it will start a fight. But I can't help myself; her anger can thrill me sometimes.

Tess feels unsettled and vaguely angry

I can tell I am driving my mom insane. She hates the way I am emphatic, determined, even in my sighs. The way I can slap a glass down on the kitchen counter or table. The way I step hard on the cement floor so there is a little pound with each step. The way I leave a little something everywhere I go—a scrap of paper, a bra, a towel. You can see her shiver at the shoulders a little. Oh, well. It's not that I don't care; it is more like I don't have the room to care.

My mind races. Not in an ADHD way, where you are easily bored. I believe I am driven by hope and expectation—and they can both be loud. About a week ago, I bought some weight-loss powder. It is legitimate. I did lots of research on the internet. Also the powder has amino acids and electrolytes. There are some of us in the world who need to work from the outside in, and what that means is this: Let love filter in like the sun does when you are cold and have found a patch of warmth on the back porch, and you stay there. It means let the rain wash away every bitter expectation that was there for the garden and the trees. We don't assume the rain and sun will ask forgiveness for their successes or failures, do we? I want to be improved or destroyed by things from the outside: a boy, my looks, teachers. That way I can know some things to do: move, change eyeshadows, don't study math. This type of reasoning makes my mom's head shake in a sort of disbelief. Not like she thinks I am dishonest or a liar. More like I am from another planet. This aggravates me that my own mom does not get me.

I am so disappointed. It is taking much longer than I wanted to reduce my overall appearance. After the powders, I decided to give myself highlights in my hair, and that was disappointing—they were uneven. Hope weighs a lot and disappoints a lot, and that is the bang my mother hears when I am struggling and walking through the house or even through the world. I am entitled, I think, to protest a little. That is why I slam the brush down on the bathroom counter. I am disappointed about the brush, the highlights. How little difference it makes. Why not be mad?

Soon I will enter my second year in high school. I know this worries my mom. She said that she read this is an important time for girls—that I will be confronted by those who use drugs and have sex. She may have read this. I also know, though, that in the back of my mind and hers is the fact that Jake began to use his second year. But I have no interest in any of that. I am interested in friends. I am interested in some guy that I don't know or only know a little coming up to me and saying, "You are really pretty." That is all—no more, no less. I cannot tell this to my mom.

I tried to tell my aunt Debra, but she was only a little better than I think my mom would be. She said something like, "The bad news is that the boys will walk away, but you will always be with yourself, so you might as well try to like the fact of you." I don't really like that. In fact, I hate that. How many people have a dad who loses touch with reality and believes he is part of God's army? If I am alone with myself, that is what is sung to me over and over again. I can't ignore the fact the way Jake did with drugs or become a nerd the way Mia is. But I can be loud and look at my mother in a very sullen manner. I know at some point I might need to calm down about the facts of my life. But before I do, aren't I entitled to an explanation—a satisfactory one? Not one that I have received so far, which basically amounts to "That sucks." But why does it suck, and when will it stop?

My mom has a nun friend, and I asked her this, and she said, "That is up to you and how soon you want to start praying." Oh, my God, there it is again, the get-quiet approach. I swear I am going to prove everyone wrong with that someday.

Last year, I got pretty mediocre grades. I am not sure I care. Let Mia and Jake be the extraordinary students. Let me be someone who is liked, not by lots of people but just three or four people. But I want them to like me in great and steady amounts. This is what I want. I am satisfied with my friendship with Lauren. Some people think she is beautiful. I do. Bright red hair and a very adult figure. I get jealous though; she is so comfortable talking in groups. I am not.

I am proud of myself and feel a little rebellious in terms of what my mom wants for me. She wants me to have bigger concerns. I know, though, that my business is me. And that my mother has only part of the information regarding her daughter Tess. Like how I want to be religious and know that there is a God watching over me. I want that as much as I want friends. I have a friend, Yvette, she memorizes passages from the Bible. She meets with people from her church after school. They discuss using the Bible for guidance. And the best way to conduct oneself in a modern high school that is plagued by drugs. But her church youth group also acknowledges that there are some low-rent cops who hang out to just be mean to people like Yvette's family because they are brown-skinned and speak both Spanish and English. Since when, I wondered to Yvette, is speaking more than one language a sin? I thought that was why we were required to take another language in high school. Yvette hugged me and said, "You are tight for a white girl." That really meant something to me. Yvette is happy and friendly. She is not one of those religious people who scorn other people's lack of faith. Her faith is for her. I like her straightforward approach. I am just not able to do that.

Ever since I was little, my mom has said, "It is more complicated than you think." She says this about almost everything. But mostly as a way to explain why our family is so weird. Today, I think I can say with some confidence that our family's lack of normalcy made my mom sad, just like it made me angry. I know this because of how happy she is that my father doesn't live here anymore, and she does not have to explain to her sister the odd things that happened—dishes in the bathtub or his concept that you could dry towels in the microwave.

She would use the "it is more complicated than you think" phrase because, well, what else could she say? One day my father is teaching my preschool class how to make pasta, and the next day he is brought home by the police for loitering too near dumpsters at clothing stores. I think she wanted all of us to believe, including herself, that these eccentricities made us interesting. She called him creative and hoped his strange behavior was part of his process.

The other day while we were in the car, I told my mother—I didn't use my mean voice, and even asked if it was OK for me to say something she could possibly perceive as unkind. "Sure," she said. I told her I was embarrassed by my dad, and I always was.

"Really?" she asked, and since she was interested, I continued.

"Well, mostly in public places, like at the beach or the mall."

"Why?" she asked, and I said, "Because of his looks." He is short and fat.

"Yeah," my mom said, "but he has good hair and beautiful eyes."

I gave her a look. I asked her, "I have wondered why you are with my father, and so has my friend Lauren. Mom, there are some people who think you are pretty, so why, I mean how, did you hook up with him?"

"Well," she smiled, "some days I wonder that—not about being pretty but why Frank and me. We did have a love of poetry in common. I did like his eyes. But all I know, Tess, is that it feels like destiny, especially the children."

I took another deep breath, and I told her another thought that I've kept to myself: "When it's been really bad with Dad, like the time he tried to break into the house and you called your brother and he was taken to the psychiatric hospital, I thought, *Why was I born?* I did not need to experience this—this is a pure and shameful disaster."

"I know," my mom said, "but did you hate it afterward when we ate ice cream in bed and I tickled your back?"

"Mom, they are not related."

"Well, maybe we suffer so we can know and enjoy not suffering. Maybe things are much more complicated than either you or I know. What I have learned about mental illness is that the part of your father's brain that is in charge is where family and fatherhood have been vacated. I don't know why or how. All I know is that it is strange and sad."

"You're not mad at me and the way I feel about Dad? Especially when he made that comment in front of my friends about how cute I used to be, but something has happened?"

"That was hurtful, I know, but you bring it up so often." That was my mom's way of telling me I am being too emphatic, that I was stuck like a CD with a scratch. "What is it that you want regarding your father?"

"I want to see him walking down the street and not care."

"How will that happen?" she asked.

"Not sure," I replied.

"How about each time he comes to your mind, you cross your fingers? That will require you to physically distract yourself."

There she goes again. I have no idea where she gets these ideas; they hardly ever work out. On the other hand, I always try them out, and they work a little, but I forget to keep it up. Besides, it is too slow.

"What if I just hoped, Mom? Hope that it happens?"

"You can do that, Tess. Hope requires some quiet time but also action. You cannot think hope."

"Not necessarily," I said. "I think hope is more like the march you made us go to last week to protest the military. I mean, there you go again, giving me weird advice."

"Weird, Tess, it is true; that is what we are. But beautiful things can be weird. In nature, what is intriguing is what doesn't work out—remember we learned that when I drove you to the field trip last year to the nature conservancy. All I am saying, Tess, is take a breath."

"I breathe all the time, Mom." I knew I was being sullen. We were quiet for a while. Partly because I was tired and partly because I was mad, I asked, "Why are you driving so badly?" When I looked over, I noticed that she was crying and biting her lip. For some reason, this really annoyed me. "I am only fifteen. I can't solve your problems."

"I am not asking you to," my mom replied. I asked her why she was crying. She told me it was a trick she taught herself when Jake was an infant. That when she wanted to yell at him, she started to cry. That way, she would not get mad at him. She speculated that it was stupid and didn't really help.

"No, I guess not," I said.

We got home, and we both shut our bedroom doors behind us. I turned music on. My mom probably lay on her bed and crossed her ankles and stared out the window; she likes to do that. I pounded on the letter G of my keyboard; it was loose and flew off and hit me in the forehead. I threw myself on the bed and hit a pillow with my fist. I had never done that before, but I had seen it in movies and thought I would try it.

It worked, and it didn't work. Until I felt really gawky, I felt fierce. "GGGGGGGGGG." It is a good feel and a good sound. That is what I determined. I am the only one in this family who is not afraid of the dark. I hate when cracks of light get in my bedroom at night. I love the dark because it is the only time I can listen to myself. During the day, my talk is always about how mad I am. At night, I have to admit, the talk is gentler. The other night, I even heard myself say, "Thank you, God, for the wind." When I tried to examine that, I thought that maybe I wasn't so fearful of change. I know this is what my family fears for me. That I hate change. Maybe those words mean I won't always be upset about my looks, my family, the details of my life.

I have not mentioned this: I was my father's favorite. I had a good time with him. He took me places, the zoo; he made good songs up. I liked his roundness when I was little. I liked the way he held my hand and pointed out unusual details about plants we saw while walking through the park. I loved when he read stories to my class. I think he and I disliked participation in the physical world. He was spooked by pools, and so was I. He wouldn't walk across bridges, and it was not my favorite thing. It is strange how great it is to feel special with someone, even if the specialness is all about what you don't like and what you fear. I don't have that companion anymore. He is so different.

Sometimes I see him reciting poems on the street corner. I watch from a distance and can even see sometimes the person I loved. Once, he looked at me and knew, I know he knew, that I was the person who was special to him. Sometimes, I randomly call him; usually I hang up when he answers. But once I said, "Hi, Dad," and he said, "Is this Tess, the special one?"

I said, "Daddy, I forgive you."

He said, "I am so proud of you." The conversation made no sense to me. He said more than I wanted when he said I was special. He said less than I wanted when he could not acknowledge he needed forgiveness.

If I were blind or a zombie and needed to be led by the living, I would want to go to the forest at night. I would want to hug a tree's rough bark. I imagine my father there in the deep forest. "Why did he betray me with his mental illness?" I would ask in the dark because I would not want to see.

"I am sorry," he would say. Once again, like everyone else, providing no real answer.

Jake has an ear infection

I had a really bad earache. Joy took me to the emergency room at 4:00 a.m. on account of the pain, which, admittedly, I don't handle well. But Joy got a little freaky and kept saying to any hospital staff that walked by, "Don't give him narcotics, don't give him narcotics; give him something for the pain, just not narcotics."

That's Joy for you. She goes straight for subtext and completely avoids context. I was in too much pain to try to explain to the baffled intern and could only manage an irritated "Mom." She was afraid that I was trying to avoid telling the doctor that I was an addict, and she gave me one of those deer-in-the-headlights looks.

"No, Joy," I said, "just tell him why." Then I tried to squinch my face from irritation to pleading. I was thinking that if I could appeal to her to remember that my sobriety mattered to me and not just her, then she did not have to be hypervigilant and that clarity would work just as well as her weird half sentences and gestures. I think Joy understood it because she took a deep breath and explained that we were a family that could not take narcotics because of addiction issues. That was nice of her to make it a family issue but probably not that necessary. I don't care that much. I was able to muster, "I have done a lifetime's worth of Percocet." So began my first medical event as a recovering addict. Turns out, this pain thing is a challenge for doctors. They want to just prescribe something, but when you are an addict, you become a teaching project—meaning about twenty million interns, doctors, nurses and more tests, even a discussion of a brain scan, to which Joy flatly said, "No, not necessary."

They settled on antibiotics and Tylenol. Because I was not going to get a brain scan, there was nothing to do but bring me home. Joy gave me her room, something she always did when we were sick. I wanted to protest, like I was too old, but I did find the musky smell soothing, and my room was very, very much the room of an ex-drug addict. Dirty and random.

When we got home, Joy said she needed to run a few errands, though I suspect she was sort of worn out from the ordeal, from me—that she needed to get away from me. I am rather obnoxious when I am sick. I sort of think it is OK to demand. Joy said she had to do a few errands, and then she called my dad and asked him to come make soup for me. He gave her a list of ingredients that he would need if he was going to make soup. This annoyed her. My father made no contribution to us, and Joy, I suspect, was irritated that he could not produce the soup ingredients on his own. But she went to the store anyway and purchased them and dropped them at home. Joy waited for quite a while for my father, but he did not show up immediately. She needed to leave, so I was alone when my father arrived.

"Daaaad," I shouted as he walked into the house. I said, "No soup, just help the pain." He did not get freaky the way Joy does. Whenever any of us gets sick, me, Tess and Mia are in pain, she kind of jumps and rubs her fingers through her hair and says, "Oh, my God, oh, my God. Here, should I try to touch it? Sometimes prayer can help just by distracting you." It is the only time she gets actually religious, and it is a little freaky.

What my dad did is say, "No soup. OK, and I had a bad night." Then he proceeds to tell me that he needed to counsel someone in the halfway house that he lives in because she was depressed, and this made him think he should become a counselor. He thought with his cooking and counseling skills, there would be a great market. He understood, he said, and he did want to be of help. He would be unique, with his theoretical knowledge of Marxism, his own mental demise, and his ability to soothe with cooking.

But when I told him I was in pain and did not need food, he said he was tired, too, and within five minutes he was asleep on Joy's bedroom floor. This annoyed me, and I started to call Joy because I really wanted someone to pay attention to me. I wanted someone to care about the pain.

If I were more normal, not the self-centered addict that I have learned I am in rehab, I might have known, as my sponsor pointed out later, that Frank falling asleep on Joy's floor was insensitive. Joy was trying hard to extradite herself from Frank, but he kept returning like a bad penny. This was an opportunity for me to protect Joy somehow, but what I cared about was my pain. I didn't protect her. Once again, I did not protect her.

So I called Joy, and when she answered, I said, "Mommmm."

"Jake, what is it?"

"The paaain. I hurt; come help me."

"Where is your father?"

"Asleep on the floor." It was like I could hear her shake her head in disbelief.

She came home and put me on the couch. She warmed up the eardrops and put them in my ear, which felt good. She massaged me a little and then said, "Excuse me." She went into her room. I heard her speak to Frank: "I am sorry, but I must ask you to leave. OK?" That kind of ruined it—that question at the end. She always does something like that, especially with Frank. No matter how annoyed she is, no matter how much advantage she believes Frank has taken of her, she is still very concerned about hurting his feelings. It's weird.

When I was feeling better and my girlfriend left town, I did meet my father for lunch. Joy used to encourage us getting together. She even suggested conversation topics after I asked her what we would talk about. Joy said he is good on the topic of his great-grandfather Wright, who fought in the Civil War even though he was a Quaker and didn't believe in war but hated slavery so much.

"My ancestor Grandfather Wright had to betray his religion. Can you imagine?" Frank said. My father explained that the records in his family Bible told how Great-Grandfather Wright, after the Civil War, moved one state west each year until he got to an island off of Washington State and opened a grocery store.

I guess it was my father's use of the word "betrayal" that got to me. I have had to study it quite a bit in rehab. I've betrayed people, but Grandfather Wright betrayed a religion; it seems so vastly different. I got to thinking about

Frank and me, how we each betrayed each other because we were out of our minds. Me with drugs and Frank just because that is the way it is, I suppose.

One thing about the parents of addicts that baffles me is that they are so taken by surprise by the addiction. Yet, in my family, you just scratch the surface, and you can see addiction at every glance. My grandmother, my mother's mother. I am guessing my mother, who shudders when offered a drink, like she is remembering something, something dark. When I ask her about it, why she's scared of drinking, she just shakes her head.

At times during rehab, I wanted to, but I didn't, I wanted to get in touch with Frank and ask why earlier in the year, whenever I asked, he was willing to buy me pot or alcohol. At first I thought it was cool. But because of rehab, I am not proud of that at all, and in fact it is embarrassing. No other addict had a parent like Frank; they were closer to Joy's type. By that I mean the denial thing. And was that any better than my father's behavior? Joy was clueless as we passed bongs around, or she would go insane—kicking me out of the house, throwing things.

Besides, Frank didn't know I was a giant drug user. That I was stealing his drugs from his hospitalizations. That his sleeping pills, when crushed and smoked with marijuana, give a great high. How one night my friend Andy and I took one of everything in his drawer and walked around the city—we swore we were seeing the light spectrum bend. We walked and talked and then vomited and passed out in the bushes of the Carmelite monastery, and in the morning we went to Frank's house, that's where Joy thought we were all along, and told Frank we needed pot. We didn't tell him how dangerously high we were and how we needed help in coming down. And he got it for us.

So you can see there is enough betrayal to go around. I wonder if Joy would agree with that statement. She would say that that was one descriptive word—one of many that could be used. Joy is not about one feeling or emotion; she packs them all in. Especially when she is angry. I have been, for instance, a betrayer, a hater, a manipulator. This was the litany delivered to me after she learned I had taken her car out without permission. I don't even have a license. Boy, though, she was a bit much.

My dad. I know that I could love him and forget the mishaps, his and mine. I guess he has a girlfriend now, someone he met in the halfway house he lives in. Joy sort of rolls her eyes at this news. "I know," she said. "Your father told me."

My father lives life in bunches—a pile of good news here, a pile of bad news there. He moves between each pile, but each time the pile is the same height and grandeur; it just has different materials. For my father, sometimes, I think we kids are constantly new to him, and that must be a pleasure—one I would never wish on anyone—of mental illness. The mind moves constantly for my father, but nothing quite sticks.

I have to admit Frank is bad on decorum. Joy was OK about his girlfriend news until I told her the other thing my father said: "She's a pill popper." That might have been it for old Joy. This time, she did not cry or look sad as she shut the door behind herself to call him. I have no idea what they talked about, but I am going to guess she forbade him from coming to the house because, after the phone call, she had that determined look. It is rare but one she is trying to cultivate, I think. Especially now that she is going to meetings about having an addict in the house.

My aunt supposes that Joy told Frank that his violation was grave. My aunt says Joy may seem fragile at times, but when it comes to children, she is willing to turn anything into a weapon if she thinks it will protect them.

My father has not been in touch since Joy closed the door. He used to call at least once a day. I love my father, and I wish his insanity were rarer and more predictable. That our lunches together could be dependable, not about me gathering stories for my friends but about my father loving me, that I was more than a location he pauses at from time to time.

Joy, Mia, Tess and me, we are like landmarks for him, and when he is not too crazy, he can stop and take in the view. I know that Joy used to be OK with his brief pauses, but my drug stuff has really shaken her up. Ever since the pill-popper talk, Joy insists that she be involved in the conversations or visits any of us has with Frank.

I think this is kind of stupid. But I understand Joy's motive; we have that in common—the realization that we have succumbed from one disaster to the next. We have settled for a rowboat and hope—hope that somewhere there is a shore.

Mia remembers

There is a picture of me my mom loves. I know because she tells me at least once a week. She'll tap the glass on the frame and say, "Gosh, how I love that picture of you, Mia."

There is nothing magnificent about the snapshot. I am three, holding a Groovy Girl doll. I have on a purple dress (I lived in that dress) with green pears on it. I have no shoes, only socks. My hair, as always, was not combed. I am staring very directly into the camera. I remember the situation vaguely.

We had just moved into the house, and there was no furniture. Jake and I used the tiled floors as a skating rink—running and then sliding in our socks. The goal was to glide on the floor for as long as possible. I was good—better than Jake, and he still let me play with him. Being better than Jake at any sport or game could be problematic.

The other thing that was pretty fun was my Groovy Girl dolls. My mom was sort of proud of me because Groovy Girls were plain-looking. They were Raggedy Ann-type dolls, but they had wild hair and really modern clothes—no prom dresses for these ladies. What I liked was that you could change their clothes quickly and often because their limbs were very flexible. My mom liked to browse in the bookstore that sold the Groovy Girl dolls, and I would play with the whole array of dolls, all slightly odd in their unique way. The owners didn't seem to mind my removal of the dolls. I was always careful to return them, and I could generally count on my mom to either buy clothes for the dolls that I had at home or sometimes a whole new Groovy Girl doll.

I think my father was a bit annoyed that my mom and I were such a team. Once I heard them arguing, and he was saying that my mom was overprotective of me because we were both the youngest in our respective families. "Don't oversimplify," she said. I didn't know what that meant, but somehow I felt she had defended me.

Have you ever noticed that kids can make an argument either way? Why they are their parents' favorite kid and then the next day argue they are the least favorite and, therefore, are being treated badly. It just depends on their mood. Sometimes I think I can argue that Jake is the favorite kid because my mom spent so much time with him on homework. I can also argue that Tess is the favorite because she and my mom take long walks together, or my mom is willing to drive Tess and her friends anywhere. I can even argue that I am a favorite because my mom and I can lounge together—lie on her bed and read our separate books together, not talk.

I could also make a case that I am the only one who did not get to see my father as sane. I just do not recognize the stay-at-home dad Jake and Tess describe. My father took them to school and picked them up. I remember it was my mother who drove me to Montessori preschool. I wonder about this now. Maybe she knew by the time I started school that the real world was getting hard for my father. His distractions, thrift-store runs, his need to leave us to look for family members in the Northwest were increasing. My mom must have decided what part of the real world he would do. Driving us around started to make her nervous. She must have decided that he would be part of the family by cooking for us. Because I remember that, even till the end, he would cook.

On Saturdays, it was Tess, my mom and me who had lots of fun. We would go to open houses and pretend that we were extremely rich and that we needed at least five houses because we had so much fancy furniture.

Tess would say, "I am not sure that my gold sled bed would fit in here." And my mom and I would look and imagine the imaginary bed in the space she was referring to. And depending on what our imaginations said, we would agree or disagree. Afterward, we would share two bean burritos instead of buying three.

My father loved music and liked to sing. But in the car, he listened to talk radio. In fact, he hated listening to music on the radio. I wonder about that now as well. Perhaps he only wanted music if he could listen closely and absorb it. Sometimes I fear he was sad and mad because my mom and their friends were just not that interested in his musical theories or his knowledge of obscure jazz classics. He seemed sullen in the car, and I would suggest that maybe music would be a better choice than these weird talk shows about people confessing that they had been taken up in spaceships. He just ignored me. My father and I, we just never had the opportunity to click, especially after his father died.

When my father moved out, when I was in third grade, he would spook me. The days were short, and it would almost be dark when I came home from school. He would be on the front porch smoking. He would barely acknowledge me and continue to sit. I would leave him there, enter the house and lock the door. We all did that. My mom and brother and sister used the side door so they would not have to see him. Eventually, he would get up and leave.

The other spooky time was when he would pound on my mother's bedroom window in the middle of the night with a poem or a song he had just written. It was always hard to tell if my mom was profoundly concerned or very angry. I suppose both. I love my mom, but sometimes I think it was a great disservice that she tried to make our weirdness normal. That she tried to make my father's behavior "interesting." It was not.

My mother has given up on the concept—the concept that we are a family that is differently organized and things are a lot better. Now my mom won't let my father inside the house. I think after the day he tried to break in at my aunt's house—the day my mom lost her job—she was done with the family reorganization.

It used to be that my father would come over and prepare meals, and we would sit in the dining room, and my mom would say that each of us had to tell one thing that happened during the day. Now I have more permission to keep to myself. We hardly ever have a meal in the dining room but cram together at the small table in the kitchen. There is a lot of reaching and a lot less passing of the food. I like it better.

You know how they say some people wear their hearts on their sleeve? My father wears his imagination on his sleeve. Especially after the first hospitalization but before the third one. My mom did not let him come over after the third hospitalization. I can tell you about that in a moment. We heard every idea and thought he had. He was talking all the time.

He had an idea on how we could get rich—by buying clothes from a thrift store and selling them on the internet. He would bring clothes over to our house, I guess, in the middle of the night and would hide them in the backyard. He didn't have space at his place and didn't understand why my mom would not embrace his concept. He said he had no choice but to hide them in the backyard till he could prove to us all what a good idea it was, which he never did.

Another idea was to write his autobiography in rhyming couplets. And then he wanted to teach poetry to poets—to famous poets—poets who had forgotten the struggles and form. Something like that.

The reason my mom refused to let him into the house after his third hospitalization: She learned, and even I am ashamed to admit this, he sometimes would buy Jake marijuana and alcohol. That was basically it. She no longer finds any sympathy for him. The day she found that out, she filed for divorce.

I hope he is healthy and happy, but that is all. I am not sure what I would do if I knew either way, the good or the bad. Either way, I think my question would remain the same: Do we matter to him? It has been almost six months since I have seen him. Every time I am asked do I miss him, I am emphatic when I say no. In fact, I have asked my mom to quit asking me. However, I have to admit I can be curious about him and filled with a great many what-ifs.

One of my what-ifs is: If I could have different parents, would I? If I were allowed to pick those parents, the answer would be a definite yes. I would definitely want my mom's friend Angela, if I could. Her house is nice, she is not spacey like my mom and I never get tired of talking to her. What would that be like to come home each day to my mom, Angela, eat crackers and cheese in a very clean kitchen and discuss the day? But what if I couldn't pick my parents? It could be very bad indeed.

The other day, I did talk to my mother about my genes. It was a class assignment for my science class. Why do I look the way I do? Now, my investigation would freak Tess out. She would be scared that she got too much of Frank's genes or that she would learn of some hidden abnormality. She might imagine that she is going to have to learn that all her fingernails are going to fall out at a certain age, or she has a genetic disposition to fear Europe.

I decided after speaking to my mom that I probably have quite a bit from her side of the family, looks and interest. However, I was able to say that my proportions come from my father. Tess would never admit such a thing.

I wish I could say that my family's problems were normal. Even losing your job could be normal, but in my family it has to include my dad's mental illness and my brother's drug use. I wish my troubles did not involve my father talking to God and that God wanted to shake down our house. These are things you just are not going to share with your friends at school. My mom says that we have an interesting life. I know she hates it too. She pretends each day can be successful by being normal. "See, the sun came up," she will say.

But I notice she sometimes puts her sunglasses on after making her comment. What I want to say is, "Mom, I know that at some point during the day you are going to cry your eyes out. So don't think you are clever by putting on your 1970s sunglasses—granted, they are making a comeback." But what I do say is, "Mom, is there anything interesting for lunch today?"

1986
Joy makes history, part 2

Two weeks after my conversation with Mark, my best friend, Roxanne, drove me to the abortion clinic. On the ride over, I told Roxanne how Mark had given me one hundred of the three hundred dollars I had asked for and that I didn't know why I had settled for that. At the time that I asked him, I was unsure even of what the price tag was for the abortion, but I thought three hundred was fair, and now I was mad at myself for agreeing on the one hundred because of what I still owed even after the insurance.

I also talked about learning about Renee's name and how difficult it was to actually comprehend that I was a third party in Mark and Renee's relationship. I had never considered how my actions were unkind and damaging for all of us. I was in charge of the damages here. I could have said no, and I could have not drunk too much, and I could have stopped the affair but didn't. Why? Because I knew, with a shudder of horror, that it was my imitation of what adults did. They damaged themselves, and they damaged others, and they wore those battle scars. The damage was done and the battle scars received, but I still had no idea how to proceed. My idea of myself as, at the very least, a kind person was now gone, and I had nothing to replace it with except immense fear.

"Does he know that he could be in legal trouble?" Roxanne asked. "You could make a stink."

"Oh, I don't know," I said wistfully. "I mean, I get there was a violation of the power thing. But I was the one who drank too much the first time. And I was not dragged into the following situations. I was intrigued and bored by him. I could not reconcile the ambivalence, and it got me in trouble. Besides, I have done enough damage to his girlfriend. If I went public, it would only increase her horror. I can't save Mark or me, but maybe I can save Renee."

"I am just saying you have options here on how to handle Mark," Roxanne suggested.

"I can't. I can't face having anything to do with him," I said. "I am so glad he is leaving." What I did not tell Roxanne was that I would not report Mark because I wanted the full responsibility for the pregnancy and abortion.

As we drove into the clinic's parking lot, we drove past the posters of unborn babies and canned screams. Roxanne said, "Too bad you had to go and get knocked up during the Reagan and Bush regime."

I smiled and said, "There I go again, the queen of excellent timing." I was only half-joking. I had often felt I was in the wrong moment. As the youngest of four, I was neither wanted nor enjoyed by my mother. Though my two brothers and my sister knew times when our mother had not succumbed to a love of alcohol, for me it was the consummate memory of childhood. My sweet older brother Jim raised me, and he was a devoted Catholic. I would never tell him about my current predicament, and this is the only thing that gave me a sliver of hope: That my brother would not need to know this. I would keep from him that I was careless and unkind and pregnant.

When the nurse called me in, I begged her to let Roxanne be with me. This surprised both of us—we had not discussed this possibility. Roxanne looked puzzled, as did the nurse. "Please," I said to both of them. "I read once the importance of eye contact of a loved one during childbirth. Doesn't it make sense that contact is also needed during an abortion?" The nurse and Roxanne looked at each other, and like an excellent soldier willing to march into battle thinking only of friends, Roxanne nodded her head in agreement.

The nurse told me to take my clothes off from the waist down. I said OK and proceeded to take my shirt and bra off. Roxanne gave me a quizzical look and then laughed. "Here, let me help you because you have done the exact opposite of what the nurse told you to do. How are they going to give you an abortion with your bra and shirt off but your pants on?"

Roxanne sat on the floor and grabbed and pulled from the cuff and bottom of my pants. We spent a few minutes pulling, tugging and laughing. Finally, I was ready.

After the abortion, Roxanne bought me a milkshake, and we drove to the top of a hill. Every city has this hill—the one where lovers or those in despair go to view the lights from above. And the lights for each have different meanings. For those in love, the lights are jewels shining for each embrace. For those in despair, the lights are like a scattered and discarded idea. Hope was my discarded idea.

It was November. Roxanne asked me how my mother

was. My mother had started chemotherapy just three weeks before. "She gets tired," I said flatly, "but is kind of hoping that her hair will grow back thicker."

"Did I ever tell you that my mother had an abortion? But this was in the late 1940s, so she went to Mexico," Roxanne volunteered.

"Can you imagine? How frightening," I responded, momentarily grateful that my abortion did not require that kind of surreptitiousness, planning, expense, fear and danger.

Roxanne continued, "In spite of how difficult it was, my mother says that she never regretted that abortion. She says that she was happy, eventually, at the life she had. That she loves my brother and me and she does not give us that weird wondering look you see in some women who are so full of regret."

"Are you trying to make me feel OK about this decision?" I asked.

Roxanne replied, "Is it working?"

"Yes."

It was working. Roxanne could do just about anything, and it would work, I often thought.

Roxanne's auburn hair fell softly in waves around her face. Her darkness and calm intrigued me—I often felt burdened by my own features: large eyes, broad shoulders and big face. Roxanne was different, contained. But while I admired that containment—to me, it was self-possession—I learned that for Roxanne, it was a source of frustration. In her eyes, the containment was fear.

I asked Roxanne, "Are you angry with me?" And she asked why she would be. "Because I am stupid," I ventured.

To which she responded, "I am annoyed that you don't

have better taste in relationships. I mean, you have so much to offer; why would you go for the callow types?"

"What does *callow* mean?" I wanted to know. Roxanne admitted she might have made the word up, but in this instance, it meant a cross between shallow and calloused.

"I can drink to that," I said, and we toasted our milkshakes. When it was dark, Roxanne started the car and headed down the hill to drop me off. She was apologetic, telling me she would have stayed, but she was starting a new job working with the mentally ill and needed to get home—a forty-minute drive to a different city.

I had left the small attic apartment, the one I brought Mark to. My new apartment was an attic as well. But I fell in love with it because it had a clawfoot tub that looked over the Cascade Mountains. Because the doctor told me not to take a bath for the next two weeks, I sat on the bathroom floor with its art deco tile and stared out the window. Then I got up, gathered a pillow, blanket and candle, stepped into the empty tub fully clothed and lay down. I was hoping for a feeling— sadness or relief.

I thought about the day and the picket lines and the procedure, which was loud and painful, and how I had asked to see what was removed from me. I saw the smallest glob; *a thumbnail*, was my immediate thought. It was then that I determined that I was going to allow everyone to be right. That indeed I was killing a life and was also saving a beloved soul from a stupid, horrible life. I thought about my anger and bad attitude toward my Catholic background but also the beauty of its art and spirit of forgiveness that had saved me many times. I wanted to understand, to genuinely know, that the thirty-minute procedure would have an effect on me for the rest of my life. And I didn't want to cry because I wanted to know that there was no use in that. From the tub, I looked out at the blackness. I knew the Cascades were out there, a bulk that was present but not seen. Eventually, I dozed off.

I awoke to my sister Debra's phone call. On the same day I learned I was pregnant, I had gotten the news that my mother had cancer. My first thought was that it was a trick—that my mother always needed to have the upper hand in family dramas. But then I talked to my father, whose sad and worried voice convinced me that things were very serious. I was unemployed. I had already quit my waitress job just that week, two days before the abortion. I got off the phone and called my brother Jim and borrowed money and immediately made reservations to visit my mother in Tucson.

I had two days before I left, and even though I was still bleeding from the abortion, I decided to go for a walk. I had a favorite place to go, though the walk would involve a steady climb. I bundled up; it was November in Seattle, and after being there for four years, I finally understood the need for layers, rainproof shoes and hats that could be pulled over my ears or folded into a pocket when and if the sun suddenly appeared.

My destination was a restaurant called the Surrogate Mother; they made massive chocolate-chip cookies. I timed my walk to make sure I was able to get one right out of the oven. I slowly ate one cookie, letting it melt on my tongue, and then headed to Saint Patrick's, a beautiful church in central Seattle. I loved its darkness and warmth. I sat there, still waiting to feel, even if just for a moment. Some sadness, fear, relief. Still none. The closest I came to feeling was reciting an Emily Dickinson poem that I had memorized—the first two lines: "After great pain, a formal feeling comes / The Nerves sit ceremonious, like Tombs."

When my sister Debra picked me up at the airport, my first question was "How bad is Mom?"

"Very bad," was the reply. "Eight months to a year. She was so ill yesterday. And after just two chemo treatments, she says she does not want to go back; she is too tired, too ready to die. The doctor indicated that was the right decision as chemo would not help much while making her very sick. But Mom is being ironic as always, saying that she thinks the pope willed her to have cancer of the ovaries because she only had four children."

Debra also told me on the way from the airport that she and her husband had decided to give up trying to be pregnant. It had been nearly eight years of trying. I cringed a little with this news and held tightly to my own waist and thought briefly of my own easy conception.

I ran into my mother's arms when I got home and began to weep. I knew I should be comforting my mother, but I wanted my mother fiercely. Her pats on the back and her saying "there, there" were comforting. I promised myself that this would be it; I would take my mother's comfort one more time, and after that I would provide it to her, my dying mother.

We quickly developed a routine for the two weeks I was there. My mother still wanted to make coffee for my father—"my husband," she said with ownership. While she was doing that, I would do chores, go to the grocery or drugstore. My mother would take a nap. When she woke up midafternoon, I would sit with her while she dictated letters to old friends, her grandchildren and children.

Each would say, "I am dying. But I do not want to leave this earth without telling you how sweet you have been." Then she would report a small detail or narrative about the person she was writing to. In the early evenings, my mother and father would sip vermouth. I was a little shocked that my mother was still willing to drink even as I noted that her easy fall into drunkenness disappeared with her age, or was it her illness?

Debra and I would make dinner—comfort food, Debra said. Many nights, we had mashed potatoes and soup or hot cereal with cocoa. Strange menus, and yet we all exclaimed how wonderful the meals were.

In the evenings, Debra and I would clean up and remember stories. Then we would discuss what would happen to our father, Dan.

"Can I move him to Seattle with me?" I pleaded.

"Of course not. You have no job, no money. You are preparing for graduate school. I will take care of him. You know that I was his favorite. I have a job, and besides, it will help Robert and me through the loss of having no children."

I started to cry. "I have no children either. He loves me too."

Debra said, "Don't be insane. He is not moving to Seattle."

"I just need to cry about that for a moment," I said, breaking into gulping sobs.

When I landed back in Seattle, Roxanne picked me up at the airport. In a disembodied voice, I gave her the report.

Roxanne was quiet but held my hand. This was another thing I loved about Roxanne: I was able to be quiet, especially when the situation could not be described. We drank tea in my apartment while sitting on the floor.

"What are you going to do?" Roxanne asked.

I looked at her to seek clarification. "What do you mean?"

"Are you in any shape to start graduate school? It starts in four months, and your mother will be declining."

That stopped me. The logistics of my mother's fall into illness and my career as colliding universes had not even occurred to me.

"Wow, I don't know. I mean, in a stupid way, graduate school is what I need for money. They are going to pay for the tuition and have me teach."

"I know," said Roxanne, who had received her graduate degree in psychology in the previous term. "But I am here to tell you graduate school is consuming, and I didn't even have papers to grade like you will. Why don't you go talk to the chair of the department? I can go with you if you want."

There was nothing else to do but follow instructions: I did as Roxanne told me. I asked her to go with me. She said she had the next day off and could go then. And so we went, walking together to the chair's office.

"Thank you for meeting with me, Professor Dolan." I told him the story of my mother's illness but skipped the part of the narrative regarding Mark, who shared a place in my lineup of disasters.

Professor Dolan agreed to let me start a semester later and promised to even keep my money intact.

I got a job in a small bookstore near where I lived—a

bookstore with a rare-book room. It was a job more appropriate to someone younger, I would think as I prepared for work. Then I would realize, "This is a job for someone who has no place to go, kind of like me." I figured I would work in the winter and spring, take the month of April off to be with my mother and then begin my graduate studies in the summer session. "Please make her last that long," I said each day as I walked, almost marched, to work.

Every Saturday night, Roxanne and I would have dinner—it was my only social interaction. I did not notice my transition into isolation. That I had quit going to movies, meeting friends for coffee, discussion groups—that I had let all that fall away from me with barely a thought. Roxanne remained the constant. She began to ask worriedly if I knew that I was rail thin and my skin was constantly chapped. She would ask me, but I was unaware and always felt at a loss when asked to consider anything that might imply the existence of my body.

Later in the evenings, I would call my mother, hoping for reports of good days. Once my mother said that she felt good and had even gone to participate in her aerobics class. Once she reported that she was able to raise her arms a couple times.

"Mom, that is fantastic," I said.

She shot back, "Don't get your hopes up. I, I am dying." And whenever she would say things like that, I felt like I was being accused of some unnamed crime.

"Was I too cheerful? I just wanted to be encouraging," I wrote in my journal. And then, "I used to want to announce very simply that my mother did not love me. Hated me for being born and complicating her life by being one more thing she needed to take care of. Now I think we are the proverbial ships in the night. She did love me, and I loved her, and it was absolutely the wrong kind of love I needed to thrive or even be part of the world."

I had trouble sleeping. I started to take long walks in the late afternoons to help prepare me for sleep. It got so that I would walk up to five hours an evening, returning at one in the morning, exhausted and able to sleep till I needed to be at work at 10:00 a.m. The walks might have been intriguing and romantic during a different period, the cold air seeping through my semi-bundled body. On some nights, the sky was orange at the horizon, and each star a little mouth with all the world's finished stories. I was walking and wanting to throw my stories up to the stars, but I could not. My stories were incomplete.

Joy tries to talk to her friend Angela about her brother Jim

And now I was a mother. I didn't drink, but I had my own peculiarities. Maybe my attachment to Sister Joan Clara was one of them. Shortly after my talk with her, I got together with my friend Angela. This particular visit needed to have a specific purpose, I explained to her. "This nun that I see, Sister Joan Clara, says I need to talk about how sad I am that my brother Jim died." Then I said, "I am very sad." And Angela said, "OK."

The next thing out of my mouth was: "Do you remember when we were young, before I moved to Seattle, and we would go to the bar called the Merry Widow?"

Angela responded with, "Sort of. Why?"

I was not sure why I had asked. "I guess I was just wondering if it was still around."

Angela said, "I don't know, probably not. But why are you wondering?"

"Because I think about it" was all I could come up with.

"In relation to Jim?" Angela inquired.

"No," I said. Angela was always supportive but a little out

of her league with my non sequiturs. She gave me a quizzical look.

"Sometimes I am embarrassed because everyone dies," I offered. "Remember our friend Tony who killed himself in his dorm room, and you were so mad and thought he was selfish. But I was stuck on his timing. Was it his time to go? I wondered. I wondered because I always hoped and believed that if you had to die, maybe God would let you die when you wanted to. Like it was some deal you could negotiate with God. But my brother Jim really did not want to die, and he was the best person I knew."

Angela was always able to muster up her own memory as a way to be a good friend to me. "I remember how angry my mom was," she said now. "My mom was told she had six months to live, and then one week later my dad drove her to a doctor's appointment, and in the doctor's office he had a heart attack. He died three days later. My mom was so angry; she thought he died on purpose so he wouldn't have to watch her being sick."

I shook my head slowly. I, too, remembered the event. How Angela and I stood in the parking lot of the hospital. It was hot and sticky, and the sky was confused, not knowing whether to rain or to beat the two of us with sun. It was like the sky was a bruise above us. I tried to smoke a cigarette like Angela was doing, even though I had never smoked before. I coughed and sputtered, allowing Angela to laugh hysterically at my ineptness. I remembered it as one of the few times I was able to perform a good-friend duty—letting myself be laughed at like that, helping Angela through that moment of her father's death. I remembered all of this as we sat on Angela's elegant, comfortable bed.

Angela was still trying to figure out why I had traveled across town to have this conversation, three years after Jim died. She asked, "Why does Sister Joan Clara want you to talk about Jim dying?"

I grabbed a pillow, hugged it and said, "I'm not sure. I think maybe she thinks I cry so easily about it that it signifies distress. But I don't think I will ever cry enough."

"Maybe," Angela said, looking to inject a little levity, "Sister Joan Clara does not know that you are a big crybaby. That ant bites make you cry and when you forget to buy laundry detergent. That makes you cry too."

I laughed. "Maybe she doesn't know that. It might be about God and how I kind of gave up on the whole God thing after my brother died. Because Jim didn't get to die when he wanted to and because he is not here with me during this ridiculous crisis I am having." I think Angela assumed I was talking about Frank's breakdown, Jake's drugs and my job loss. She admitted she felt something was wrong, that she was the wrong person to have this conversation with. She told me she had been depressed only twice in her life, and she didn't like it.

I asked Angela what she did when she was blue. "Well, this might sound shallow, but I ran a few extra miles for a few extra days, and then I signed up for a marathon so I would have something to look forward to. You know, get my mind off things. Though I wasn't even sure what caused me to be sad. It was way after I was sad about my parents."

Now I was puzzled. She could get her mind off things and be a dedicated runner herself, but her own inevitable sadness followed her. I just couldn't understand her strategy. But if I was confused about Angela's ability to stare at sadness directly, she was stymied by my inability to escape depression. Perhaps she was not as complex as I, she offered. That made me laugh.

I counteroffered that she was, that it had more to do with body chemicals. And that, besides, Angela was so generous, and that required more than a simple understanding of things.

"We are not talking about Jim," Angela observed.

"Yeah," I acknowledged, "I know we are not doing the assignment, but I am OK though."

Angela was a little nervous; she said she thought it was kind of hard to talk about something you are required to. I laughed and said, "I know. Do you think it's harder when you are required to be quiet or when you are required to talk?"

"I never do anything I don't want to," Angela said. "I think, I hope, this will guarantee that I will be pleasant."

"Really?" I asked. I felt like she was getting insider information on how to be human. "Do you think that is why I am insane and you are not? I feel compelled to try to figure out what the right thing is for each occasion, as if there were some large answer, when the more useful response might be, 'Does it make me happy?' Like this very conversation. I am following the nun's instructions, and maybe I simply have nothing to say about Jim, but I feel I should try."

Angela said she was sure that I had a great deal to say about Jim and that Sister Joan Clara just wanted me to be happy. "You are not insane, just overwrought and close to insane."

This only made me wonder all the more: "Well, can I add that sometimes I am impressed that I get up each day? And what does the end of grief look like anyway? Will I quit running into walls and getting bruised? Will I remember where I have put my keys? Will I suddenly remember the words to 'Norwegian Wood'? That was my favorite Beatles song."

"Possibly those things could happen," Angela responded. "Or you might enjoy things more. You don't have to be sad."

I was not prepared to accept that. "I don't believe that. Sad is where I belong, and anything else is false. Sad means I can be true. So I get to feel and taste what I need to."

Angela just laughed. "Joy, that is kind of morbid or poetic, I am not sure which. Or maybe both. You could be sad and other things too. Could you make that compromise with me? To have some fun and joy? I think your kids might like it. Your children are wonderful and remarkable. But we owe our children our own happiness, I think. That and their own happiness."

I remembered how Jim once said, "I just want my children to call me once a week, tell me 'I am OK.' I want to not worry a week at a time; that seems fair." Jim said that to me—it was before I had children; I remember it so clearly. Then he asked me if I wanted a milkshake.

Angela asked, "Do you want a milkshake? You know, it is not that complicated. You love, you let go, you find a newness. You live and die, and in between you try to do well in all spheres—financially, emotionally, with children and friends. You know there will be war and unfairness, and you hate that, and you don't agree to participate."

I feared that Angela was losing patience with me. "I don't know. Maybe I need religion," I said.

Angela's tart reply: "If you want that."

"Do you want religion, Angela?" I asked.

"Sure, look at all the Virgins of Guadalupe that I have in my house."

"I thought that was an aesthetic decision," I said.

"How are they different?" Angela wanted to know. "God is an aesthetic." Then she laughed. "I have no idea what that means, but I thought you would like it. That it would be something you would say, Joy."

I remained serious. "I remember, when your son Jules was born, how careful you were to present the natural world or the hours of placing the crib in just the right place so Jules would always have a piece of light. And what was important to me was that my kids be protected. I am not even sure from what. I kissed and kissed their heads. Perhaps I was already concerned, without knowing it, that they would inherit my sadness and their father's insanity. It is impossible to know what will be there for them. I feel miserable about it."

Angela, too, became philosophical. "Think how interesting their lives are and the great stories. They are loved. They have been dealt cards—like all of us. Some would say they have received the gift of grief at an early age, and that is useful. Have you ever met someone who has not suffered? Their faces stay baby-like, and they are, well, intolerable."

I found myself laughing. "Angela, this does not sound like you."

Angela said, "Let's go make milkshakes." And so we did.

Mia notices that Tess begins to use the word "dude" a lot

My sister, Tess, about five months ago, started to use the word "dude" a lot. I can pinpoint the date exactly because I remember the situation very well. I remember it well because I am that type of person, but also it coincided with something I was very involved with. I was writing in my journal on January 12, 2009. I was writing a different ending to the book *Anne of Green Gables*. I thought the original ending was flawed because it was too predictable—going back to Green Gables was too easy. Maybe Anne should not have gone back to Green Gables. What would have happened if she had stayed in Brooklyn and had become urban? What if she helped people in the big city, scrubbing and making an orphanage clean for children? Maybe she should have stayed in Brooklyn and become a big-city girl. Or what about something exotic like going to the Amazon?

I also object to the way Anne is able to forgive and move on, like she did with Gilbert Blythe. Or how she was able to become "bosom friends" so effortlessly, like she did with Diana Barry. I just don't think that is realistic. In fact, I know this from experience.

I know that you can figure out the right things to say to appear that you are well-informed, but that is different from saying things because you feel the need to say them. I offer as an example the school bus. I could say I went to the mall, I could say I like a certain new video, I could say that someone is stupid or nice. This would make me "socialized," able to get along with peers. And I have done such things; I can talk this way when I want to, when I want to prove I am able to be one of the gang. It just makes me a little sad because I have to face the fact that I lack Anne of Green Gable's enthusiasm for "bosom buddies."

Anyway, Tess was on the phone with her friend Kate, and because our walls are thin, I heard her talking. At first I was confused because I thought the word "dude" only referred to boys, and Tess was saying, "Dude, do you want to shop for school this weekend?" "Dude, I want to try some of this blue eyeshadow that glistens; they have free samples at Forever 21." I wondered why Tess was inviting a boy to the mall to try on makeup. This was odd, most particularly because Tess is mainstream. Jake and I have talked about this. How she longs for clothes like everyone else. Jake thinks it is stupid. He would rather wear the opposite of the current fashion. I am made a little anxious by this aspect of Tess. I want to wear the items that are closest to the checkout stand because that means I don't have to be in the store very long. How could one want to be in a store constantly working and determining their style?

Tess is not comfortable with what is not normal, and so I was taken aback because I thought she must be talking to a boy about blue eyeshadow. I tried to find Jake to let him know that something had changed, changed drastically, with

Tess. I hoped it would please him that she was going weird on us. I had to admit I was thrilled by the idea. I thought if Tess has an unusual friend, then maybe I wouldn't bug her so much with my preference for books. I admit it. I hoped if her friend was a boy who wore eyeshadow, I would be let off the hook.

It wasn't until later, when she asked my mom to drive her and Kate to the mall, that I realized what was going on. It was Kate on the phone, not some boy who liked eyeshadow. That was when I really noticed how she used the word "dude." She called all of us that, my mom, my brother, his girlfriend. She even uses "dude" sometimes to describe things, like it is some sort of adjective. "That lipstick is dude." I have no idea what that means.

I hate it when things are not precise—when the spices get on the wrong shelf or the knives and forks and spoons get jumbled up. So using "dude" as a generic noun, especially after I understood that no boy was included, really got on my nerves. But I tried really hard not to say anything. On occasion, I have said, and only to myself, not out loud, "Tess, stop. That makes no sense—why are you trying to confuse what does not need to be confused?" Tess can give a look of full disgust, and it makes me sad sometimes, and that is why I never said it out loud.

I love Tess, but there is no pleasing her. She gets mad at me for being smart. But look at her, thick auburn hair, and I am jealous for the simple reason that she actually has a desire to go to the mall. I just turned twelve, and I cannot muster up the desire. Some of my schoolmates go, and I have been invited; I am not a total geek loser. But I feel more comfortable hanging around with a book or fan fiction on the Web or writing my own books. I don't want to venture out like Tess. I guess I am scared. I guess I have to say that.

I have come up with a term, "the successful talk between strangers becoming friends." I don't know that talk. The talk I know happens in books and is automatically clever and distinguished. You know the "frankly, my dear, I don't give a damn." That kind of talk. But who actually says things like that? So you see my quandary? (1) I don't know how to do "the successful talk between strangers becoming friends." (2) I would prefer to talk like I was in a book, even though I know that that kind of talk does not exist probably anywhere in real life.

Besides, it is not like I am completely free of desires. I even want what Tess wants: lipstick, perfume. The other day the strangest thing happened. I was at Walgreen's with my mom. I found myself touching just about everything in the makeup section: lip gloss, lip sheen, lip marker, eyeshadow, eye enhancer, eye highlighter, foundation cream, foundation powder, coverup. I kept passing my hand along the containers. I was touching, touching gently. I wanted them all, and I wanted to wear each and every item. And I wanted to wear them right then and there. It is scary for a girl like me to want so suddenly and immediately. There should have been two of me, I wanted so much. I even got a little dizzy. Then I started crying but only to myself; no one noticed . . . except my mom. She saw this, and she offered to buy me lip gloss. I knew that would be entirely unsatisfactory, so I said no.

But why? What happened to me that, suddenly, the offer to purchase me lip gloss wasn't enough? I am not a greedy girl. I share my lunches or at least am willing to do trades. I've given my friend Phil my favorite book before. So why, suddenly, if I could not have every piece of makeup did I not want any?

When Tess is lying on her back and calling everyone "dude," I am annoyed because I believe in specificity. I tried telling myself this is why just lip gloss was unsatisfactory. Lips are only a part of my face. I have other parts of my face, and it would be inaccurate to address just one area. I tried this argument with my mom on the way home, but she just gave me a crooked smile. Meaning "no go, Mia." Anyway, I knew I was not telling the real reason.

The truth of the matter is ever since I turned twelve, I am dissatisfied and want so much. I want so much: candy, clothes, bathing suits, and makeup. And the other truth is—no one I know in any of the books I read is like this. Hermione, Harry Potter's friend, wants lots of things, friends and time to do her work and spells. But Hermione is different; she wants things that are necessary. I want what is unnecessary.

The other thing—and this would hurt my mother's feelings, but it has dawned on me—is that my family provides me with no peace. They are interesting, and I know my mom tries real hard. But if I let them, they would occupy me—I could worry about my brother and drugs, my mom's sadness, my dad's craziness and Tess and her use of "dude." I could spend my time wishing for order. In fact, in all honesty, this is how I do spend much of my time. Worrying and hoping. I'm afraid I hope that we could change the things that happened. That my father didn't go crazy, that my mom did not lose her job, and Jake. How strange it is to see someone you love become a stranger.

The makeup, the wanting makeup, it was the exact feeling I have for my family. Almost there, almost mine. But I could not figure out what goes together, what eyeshadow and what lipstick match completely so completeness is there.

Recently, I asked my mom if she could make lunches, given it is summertime and an organized lunch could be in order. A lunch at home at a predictable hour. "No problem," she says. Grilled cheese every day, and she bought the cheese already shredded—that means there is no luscious lump of warm cheese when you bite into the middle. Tess or Jake might want to let her know that her grilled-cheese sandwiches are deficient, but I don't. I am just a little disappointed. I corrected and advised my mother on how to make grilled cheese. I demonstrated and showed her. She seemed sad, like she understood that it was sad for me that I was showing my mom how to make a grilled-cheese sandwich.

But there are so many people who love me. Just the other day, my aunt Debra took me to get my haircut and then invited me over for dinner and a sleepover. On my twelfth birthday, she wrote a note that said, "Thank you for showing me you can be wise at any age."

Besides, I don't know what I want. I really have no desire regarding my father, and I don't feel very bad about his mental illness. I am sure some smart psychologist would say that it was not true. They would say that, deep down, I am sad and unsure of what this means for me. They would ask me if I have any memories of my father. "One," I would say back. I would tell them about the day I learned to ride a small tricycle. That I was fast and good at going around the trees. I was best in my daycare class. I mean by that, I was fast. Someone might find it interesting that my first memory isn't about some great book I read but about some dumb tricycle. I was riding it fast, and my father walked in the gate. It must have been time to pick me up. The sun was so bright, and it was hard to make out his face. I could tell, though, it was him by his walk and fisherman's cap. I stopped suddenly when I saw him. I knew it was time. I rose from the tricycle. And that is simply it—that is my memory.

OK, so Tess has decided to call everyone "dude." I think it is strange. And, yes, it does annoy me and get on my nerves for the reasons I already said. But, in all honesty, part of me is a little proud of her. I am proud that she can break the rules a little. Breaking the rules and not hurting anyone cannot be so terrible.

Jake remembers

Joy has always appreciated that I take an interest in my father's history. However, it was not natural. I had to learn to be interested when I was about ten years old. What happened was I was visiting Joy's brother Jim, and he kept asking me about my father. I didn't know any of the answers. I did not know how many brothers and sisters he had. I didn't know what anyone's jobs were. I knew that I had met my grandparents because there were pictures of it, but that is about all.

I began to inquire more out of embarrassment than interest. My strategy was to bring it up while we were driving in our minivan. My father seemed more relaxed than at other times. My other trick was to bring it up while I was hungry and suggested we get a bite to eat. He treated me to some good ethnic food and talk. I found I was interested, after all. It was a very different family from Joy's. My dad learned after his mother died that she actually had five husbands—he thought she had three. He would wonder, "There is not much difference between three and five; why did she lie about that?"

He told a funny but, turns out, prescient story about staying with her at a cheap hotel in Seattle over Christmas.

She would buy clothes on a charge card during the day, and he would return them the following day. She also said she was channeling the angel Gabriel and Washington State Senator Warren Magnuson. Back in the day, my father and I found that amusing. But I don't find this funny anymore because of my father's own breaks with reality.

He has weird notions about music that I don't necessarily buy or even want to indulge, but I try to because it seems to make him happy. He thinks Richie Havens influenced Dr. Dre. I try to understand that and can see sometimes that it almost makes sense. Let's admit it, they are both about loneliness. Havens is sad about it and Dr. Dre angry.

I love my father, but I am not a music or an insane cohort with him like I think he would like to think. In retrospect, I am sad he shared his own LSD trips with me and that I know that he sold pot. I know it was his youth, but, still, it does not help me to relax to know that his drug use and family insanity have been around for a few generations. I mean, what does that mean for me and even my sisters?

Sometimes I wish I could make a deal with God—let it not be Mia, the one who goes crazy. She is too adorable. And she remembers having fun with me. Let that be what remains. "Why not pray for no one to have mental illness?" my girlfriend, Rose, asks. That is a good point, and probably I can't because it is something that we addicts need to learn to do. To make the deal—just one more hit and I am done with drugs. Of course, that was a deal I could never keep. But just by way of saying, I have gotten into the habit of making deals with higher powers, and so that is what I do.

I prefer my distracted stay-at-home dad who was grouchy rather than the over-the-top mentally ill person he became with age or bad medications. Unfortunately, my new dad, the crazy one, almost makes sense. I mean, it was inevitable, wasn't it? All the effort on his part to be this guy who watched and cared for us, even though he did not know what that meant. That it meant secret storage units and crazy shopping sprees and stories that were accompanied by his improvisations. "The story is better with the angle I invented for it." Sometimes I longed for a regular old narrative. A green-eggs-and-ham narration without him bursting into song or the stopping to make eggs with a dose of green dye and then being told to eat them according to his inflections on the word *egg*.

But there were excellent moments. When I was a kid, we would take bus rides to the library. Once downtown, he would place me on his shoulders and wander and point at buildings. "Is that the library?" he would ask. "Is that it?"

I never tired of saying, "No, not there. But, here, here, I found it!"

When I was a druggie, I was happy he was a character. I took friends to his house. He would throw together great meals with random ingredients. Then he would start talking about music, the blues, Mose Allison, Taj Mahal and his signature steel blues guitar. He got us interested enough so we would go back to my house and check out his references on YouTube.

My dad says it is OK to call him crazy, and that is how he refers to himself. Sometimes I will for effect with my friends, but I am sad about it. I see him suffer, but I also see he manages so well. He has people who are interested in him. Even a girlfriend with a similar diagnosis, I guess. I have never met her. I can still think about my times with him with some longing if I let myself. He is mostly in my imagination there when I listen to music. He loves music the same way I do. Joy does not love that way. She would never be able to converse with me about it the way my dad does. Frank and I are endlessly trying to follow the notes from the moment it enters the brain to the moment it reaches our fingers tapping on any surface.

My father's insanity may be beyond language. Because there are so many aspects to it. He can be thrilled to survive the day; he can be baffled about the difference between the blue and yellow pills and when to take them. There is this self-indulgence and grandiosity—my least favorite part— when he shouts his latest written "masterpiece."

Those two months before my drug overdose, my friends and I had access to his drugs, though in honesty he did not know I was stealing them. For some reason, he believes my aunt was. There were the times he would pay my friends to come over for assistance in moving his large quantities of secondhand junk from one small space in his yard to another. Then he would say we were doing it great or terrible and that we should take a break. Once he cooked a big pot of bouillabaisse, fish soup, for us on his outside grill. It was great—we could smell the seasonings; tomatoes, garlic, onion and herbs infiltrated the air, and then the fish was thrown in a dramatic way.

When he served it, the broth spilled a little with each serving and made little sparks in the air. Miles Davis in the background, overall a nice sensation. Good food and music and the sky lit with an intense red right before the sun sets. My friends and I extremely high and surrounded by my father's junk, bike parts, broken beds, dressers with missing drawers. But I don't want to go there anymore. I don't want to listen to my father's self-aggrandizement, good deals and worst of all—and only once—his erotic life with my mother.

For better or worse, it was Joy who was fascinated with me as a child. The one who celebrated my nonsensical desires: kites with embellishments making them too heavy to fly or bikes with an overkill of decorations—flags, horns, plastic flowers—making it impossible to ride. She celebrated my wanting everything and my excessiveness. Not my father. He did not think it was rational—now I see how ironic that is—and would argue with my mother about it. She would say, "But you are excessive too." He would say that Joy was indulging me. I don't know, maybe he wanted to make impossible kites too, but Joy would not help.

Maybe he was worried. Maybe he was jealous. Luckily, with my Alcoholics Anonymous program, I am learning to live just for the day. Because the future with my dyslexia, drug use and father things can look problematic. I have a feeling Joy thinks about this more than I do. She has these sunglasses she wears; my sister Mia says it is because Joy spends about a half of each day crying and talking to her sister.

My aunt—she can drive me nuts, you know; it is embarrassing to say, but she likes me too much. I can feel crowded. I know so much about Joy's family. Once a week, there is a gathering at my aunt's house, and there could be between six and sixteen of my relatives and friends. It is like verbal aerobics there. One of my cousins is always on their way or returning from some theater camp or comic workshop. I admit it is fun, though my talent is more of the contemplative type.

I like being there and can feel so lonely. I am unable to step forward. I feel I am so full of knowledge that I will burst. This is when music helps. I can arrange my room so it is cave-like. That is when I turn on musicians like Hawthorne Heights or My Chemical Romance. I like screaming. I like lyrics about rain and the cold and loneliness, and I like it shouted from the throat and guts. It is when these bands battle it out with their instruments and voices that I get some calm. Sometimes it might take hours; sometimes I need to throw in a bike ride and a cigarette. But sometimes I am aware and know that I can get to be part of some silence.

Lately, I've noticed I have been thinking about calling Joy "Mom." I have been long opposed to saying "Mom," probably because other people are so against me saying "Joy." I have always been contrary, and calling her by her first name was part of that, I know. I enjoyed the askance looks I received from adults and enjoyed Joy's perplexed look when she had to try to explain to friends this verbal aberration.

"It is her name," I replied when teachers and even friends would scold me. I automatically called her Mom while we spent so many hours in the emergency room with my ear infection. It was more efficient to call her Mom while we talked to doctors—that must have been the impulse of my decision. But I liked it—it is natural and easier.

She went ballistic about me calling her Mom, only once. The first time I was caught drinking at school. She took me out and said we have some new rules here. She was going to get to search my room any time she wanted, and from that moment on I needed to call her Mom. I loudly protested both rules and finally said, "Fuck, no, I am not going to call

you Mom." She let it go, the name one; there was no real jus-
tification.

As for searching the room, she tried. But she was pretty
pained by the whole experience. At heart, she believed in
privacy. I could not tell if it freaked her out to have to search
or fear she would find something. She didn't have the stomach for it. It diminished her. I noticed she had quietly given
it up. This was great for me. She would have never found
anything because she does not have the mind of an addict
and did not know where to look—in hats, sewn into pant
pockets, etc.

She would think, "Jake would never put drugs into my
mother's teapot; he would know how much that would hurt
me." When you are a drug addict, though, you do not think
about those things. Her grandmother's teapot was a great
place to hide drugs.

The other day my girlfriend, Rose, and my sister Tess
were chatting about a teacher at school. It was at dinner, and
we were all there. Mia and my mom too. Rose and Tess were
talking about how the teacher and her son were very close
and had lunch together every day.

Joy said, "Oh, Jake and I would be like that. We are so
close." At first I thought she was serious, and I wanted to
protest. Then I saw her face and saw she was speaking iron-
ically. That kind of hurt my feelings. In spite of everything,
I still consider myself close to her. I believe we understand
and depend on each other. Rose was talking about our relationship, and she said our success would depend on whether
or not we asked questions and said our fears.

With Joy, it is a bit different. I think we are the automobile crash sites. Our relationship is about determining the level of destructive impact we could take and still survive. I learned a body, a parent, a mother, a self can take quite a bit and not die. However, quite a bit of damage can remain. Our relationship will always have a limp and a few wounds that may not be able to form scars.

I hurt Joy the other day when I said, "Frank knows so much more than any of us, and that is why he cannot be part of us." In some ways, I believe this. But I also know Joy has been left with quite a bit of debris. But not a disease like I have or my father. My father, because of his own illness, was not terribly damaged by mine, and this in a perverse way pleases me. It is as if someone received a reprieve from me.

Tomorrow I plan to quit smoking. I wish I could say I am doing this because it would make Mia happy, but it is because Rose does not like the way I taste when we kiss. I am reading *Heart of Darkness* in English class. To me, Marlow's anguish is he has discovered secrets. As he meanders down the river and is discovering Kurtz was mad and evil and power hungry, what should he do with this information? Keep it to himself? Make something moral out of it?

The story implies there is redemption in not keeping secrets. That is what I am told in my twelve-step programs. The more secrets we give up, the better. When we were little, Joy told us that in her religion, the Catholic religion, if you said the sign of the cross when you passed a church, you would release souls from purgatory. If I start calling my mom Mom, it will be a little like that—a sign, a gesture. Perhaps I, too, can be released from purgatory.

Why Jim matters

I have never been bold. I have been demanding, especially when I am hurt. I have been clingy. I have been passionate. I can be funny. But bold eludes me. You must be loved to be bold. There was nothing particularly unlovable about me. It simply did not happen. My parents were older and tired when I was born.

There was Jim, though. He was the oldest. He discovered me when I was seven and he was fifteen. He was contemplating trying out for the high-school basketball team and solicited my help. He told me I could do anything I wanted to prevent him from making a basket. If he took a shot and missed it, I received a quarter. So I jumped and tore at him, his front and back. So began the lifelong bond between us.

Jim's thinking was this: If he could make a basket under these circumstances, it would serve him well when he was playing and his opponent actually needed to follow some rules. The strategy worked, and he made the starting team. As a reward, I was allowed to sit with Jim's girlfriend during the games.

I was pretty sure Jim's real intention in this was to prevent our mother from attending the game. I heard Jim explain to our parents that because I went, family representation was there. He didn't need to worry about our father. He would never go; he was an intellectual. Our father was not the problem.

Our mother was the problem. She was someone who could sit in the bleachers and scream. She was also known to write letters to the coaches, sort of threatening them if they did not play Jim more. Our parents agreed I would represent the family. I felt grown up going to the games with Jim's girlfriend.

Jim was very conscientious in his patronage toward me. I was relieved by this; my household scared me. My mother was loud, my sister was loud, my other brother was aerobic. Life was quieter when I was with Jim. He studied in his small room but invited me in. My only assignment was to rub his scalp when he read. Then I was allowed to "make yourself at home." I would lie on Jim's bed, cross my ankles and stare out a leaded-pane window.

When Jim married his high-school girlfriend, I felt his leaving as a great loss. My afternoons with him had been so ordinary, I felt at a loss in the house with all the excitement Debra and Michael brought in.

When I was in high school, I would go visit Jim in his new home on the Pacific Beach. He supported me when I went to school in the Northwest. When I had my own children, Jim would send for me to visit. He said he wanted me to be restored. He understood how tiring parenting could be. Because our bond was quietness, conversations could be awkward. Neither one of us knew how to speak about our worries—Jim about his health and me about my husband.

After his cancer diagnosis, I tried to visit every other weekend. He requested those visits—making me feel proud and needed. Once, he called me in the middle of the day and, though very weak, said he wanted me to know that he loved me and that I was never to forget that. I thanked him and had enough sense to not scream, "But you like being alive. You love God."

Shouldn't you get to live a long time if you love God? This was my fundamental disagreement regarding Jim's death. Sister Joan Clara wanted me to know death is not God's business, only love and free will.

When I experienced the knowledge of Frank's love, I failed to notice the possibility that my children might have his mental illnesses. Even worse, I did not really care. My hope and love for Frank mattered that much. I had moments when I thought we could fight off any mishap with our genes or whatever because of our affection for each other. Hope was my great sin, and yet I could not give it up.

1986
Joy makes history, part 3

I was getting a little worried: a hole had worn through my tennis shoes. If it rained on my walks, and it often did, water would seep in and through my socks, making my feet ache with cold. It seemed my shoes were always a little wet even though I placed them on top of my radiator every evening. All I knew was I needed this walk to the train station, but I was becoming neglectful, and winter had arrived in the Northwest. Often, I came home soaked, my fingers and toes red from the cold. I ran only the hot water and forced myself to stay in the tub till the cold had burned away.

In early February, it actually started snowing during my walk. It was on the way home from the train station that I began to notice the snow. As usual, I was unprepared for change. After ignoring the weather for as long as I could, I slipped into a pizza place in the university district to get warm. One of the creative-writing professors was sitting with graduate students. I was entering the graduate program, but I had already taken a class from the popular poet Professor Ned Blank. He liked my poetic voice and once had invited me to read at a student reading. He waved me over, and not able to think of a good reason why I should not be there, I went.

Frank was there; he had won the Creative Student of the Year Award just the previous year. He was still an undergraduate student preparing for graduate school. I knew him by reputation. He was strange-looking, chubby but with a jubilant personality and known for reciting poetry at the most random moments. I had stumbled upon that once. We were the only students crossing the University of Washington's Red Square, and Frank was reciting W. H. Auden's poem "September 1, 1939" at the top of his lungs. I acknowledged his performance but scurried past him without stopping. He did not seem to notice me.

Professor Blank said to me, "We are just admiring Frank's knife here."

"Knife?" I queried. Frank displayed what I assumed was a state-of-the-art stainless-steel knife. I was still confused as Professor Blank invited me to sit down and passed me a beer. I had not drunk since I had been with Mark. I sipped slowly.

Frank said, "Isn't it beautiful? I bought it today for friends who will be getting married. I don't think there is a better marriage gift than a knife. It has so many meanings." I found this comment cute.

"How did you learn so much about knives?" I asked.

"Cooking is my other art form besides poetry," he replied.

"Ah." I had one more sip of beer and got up to leave. I said I had transportation because I did not want anyone making a fuss about my walking in the challenging weather. Frank dug a small bottle of peppermint oil from the bottom of his coat and suggested that I put a little in a warm tub to fight the cold. I thanked him and left.

Three weeks after seeing Frank and Professor Blank and the knife, I was leaving work to start my walk. I was worried about my shoes and did not know what I would do when I had completely worn them out. As I crossed the street, I saw Frank at the bus stop. "Hi," we said to each other.

"Where are you going?" Frank asked.

"Oh, nowhere really." I was caught off-guard and unprepared to reveal my secret sojourns to the train station. "Hey, thanks for the peppermint oil. It worked. I have been cold-free."

"Great! And you should try the hot chocolate I make with it. If you have nowhere to go, come have some tea here at this café, and also they make fresh bread, can you smell it, it is just coming out of the oven." All of this in one steady sentence.

He led me into the bakery, one I must have passed a hundred times and not even noticed. I sat down, and he bought us a warm brioche and chamomile tea. With this, the strangeness of my own diet—cookies and soup—became apparent to me for the first time. I found the warm bread exquisite and filling.

I also wondered when was the last time I was this warm. The oven and coat made me toasty.

Frank said that my cheeks were pale and offered to make me curry. He lived just up the hill. I agreed, and we walked to Frank's small one-room apartment, which was messy but filled with original art done by friends.

There was a bed and an overstuffed chair. I sat down, and Frank exuberantly chopped green onions and mangoes, nuts, and threw coconut milk and spices into a pot—this was what I saw and wondered what was happening while I was watching him so full of movements. But I was unable to stare down what ingredients he was using. I believed I had never tasted anything so good. The yellow of the curry and how it burned the top of my mouth and the sweet chutney that bit through the heat. Frank beckoned me to come over and sit on his lap. I did. He used his fingers to place rice, curry sauce and vegetables into my mouth. I sucked them off. He did it again and again.

Our making love was simply part of the rhythm of the evening. Frank had precautions. And when we were done, he ran the tub with warm water, placed me in, washed my back and combed my hair. He put lotion on my very dry hands and feet. We made love again, and I never returned to the train station.

We spent a good part of a week with Frank cooking and tending to me. He found some great secondhand clothes, long skirts and playful tights. He found me soft-soled shoes that he swore were an expensive Italian brand. He showed me his horoscope from his birthday the previous August. It said, "You will get married this year." I laughed and then realized Jim would be happy: I was smiling.

I kept borrowing money from my brother Jim. He didn't mind. He loved me. He applauded my willingness to go away to college and this attempt at independence. He helped with my tuition. He also thought that I had the potential to be a famous poet if I could get over being ashamed that I wrote poems. My poems, he claimed, took the world straight on with an indictment of how we have romanticized cruelty. He would recite my lines to me: "The grace of the executioner / his darkness and muscle / his duty becoming / a grace, he hopes."

Jim had no qualms declaring me beautiful. According to him, my hair was golden with waves; I had the saddest blue eyes that would make anyone try to correct that sadness. I was at my best when I smiled or had hope.

He married a bubbly brunette. A firm believer in the possibilities of Southern California. They swam and biked, followed a number of health-food gurus. Had two children, whom they took to the beach and taught to surf at an early age. Jim stayed a firm Catholic. Much later, when he was dying from cancer, he explained to me that if you actually listened to the beliefs of the Catholic Church, it provided a wide tent. Jim said, from his bed, "You could even be an atheist and still be a good Catholic."

I would look at him puzzled. He smiled. "I would tell you more details, but right now I don't feel so well. In fact, I feel like I am dying." We both smiled at his brave irony.

I never told anyone other than Roxanne about Mark. I especially knew that it would break Jim's heart. My situation—stupidity, pregnancy, abortion—would not be anything he could possibly imagine. I believed that my situation would be harder on him than it was on me. I kept it silent.

I spoke to my mother every day. I tried not to need her. But once I broke down and said, "Mom, what will I do? I am going to miss you. We have had such a, well, fucked-up relationship.

"OK, Mom," I said, "I am sorry. I am sorry. I am sorry. Do you want me to hang up and call you back when I have pulled it together."

"Yes," I heard in a hoarse whisper, and that was the end of the call.

But, instead, I just quit calling. I had just two more weeks before I began school again. Frank continued to be attentive and kind. He brought me flowers, cooked and in the shower massaged my scalp for hours.

I had been spending the night at Frank's; no one knew about him, much less how to contact me.

It was Jim who finally got hold of me.

"Mom has just a little time left, maybe a week. I am arriving tomorrow. Why don't you do the same? Look into the tickets and call me back so I can purchase one for you."

I called Frank right away. He made my travel plans and packed a picnic for me: fresh mozzarella, a baguette and chocolate.

Mia loves the maps
of ancient Greece

Ancient Greece, in spite of the no-girl thing, fascinates me. The art and archeology and the structures. But mostly it is the water, or what I imagine to be the color of the water, and the trees—olive trees can be almost shimmery when they are close together, but if you look at one just by itself, it can be dull. Isn't that strange?

I would be lying if I don't admit to imagining living in ancient Greece and making things right for girls. Sometimes in the daydream, I use my wit, and Aristotle has to take me as a student because I am so smart, and I say, "Only if all girls can." Or I dress up as a boy and am an amazing runner, and when they discover I am a girl, they decide all girls can do sports.

For seventh grade, I have started in a new school for the "intelligent and curious" because my mom does not want me to get a big head. She says I fit into the "curious" category. In fact, she says, "You are getting curiouser and curiouser every day." Another day, another attempted joke by my mom.

The good thing is no one treats me like I am special. Though some teacher came up to my mother and said enthusiastically, "You're Mia's mother?" And that was annoying because I don't want people knowing that much about me, but I guess someone knowing who is your mother is inevitable.

The maps we see of ancient Greece are on the internet at Harvard or something. It is not as wonderful as actually touching them, but you can see how cracked and yellow they are. My teacher will gently trace a coastline with his finger and say, "You have seawater, no fresh water, and rugged terrain. What are you going to do? How are you going to survive?"

"Fishing and olives," many of us shout out, not just me. Maybe what I love is the possibility of being alone, and yet, because the night sky is so full of stars, it is impossible to feel alone.

A few weeks ago, I rattled off at school, saying the answers, and then I was so embarrassed. Afterward, though, another new girl, like me, named Jess, seemed to notice I was embarrassed. She came up to me and said, "I really admire your knowledge and politeness."

I was so surprised and then embarrassed again. But I was able to stammer a thank-you and a question about what brought her to this school. She said she had been home-schooled, but her parents got divorced, and the judge ordered her to attend a school. Apparently, my new school, named Wisdom Elementary and Middle School, seemed to be the best choice to Jess's mother. Her mother would continue to supplement the school's rigorous but secular curriculum with religious studies. Jess is religious but not at all preachy. She doesn't try to convince anybody of anything. However, she can stare down any person who teases her about carrying a Bible. We have been cautiously speaking to each other, sharing our interests and where we have traveled or want to travel. It has been fun.

And Jake talked to me again last night at dinner. Music. Bob Marley and his influence on hip-hop.

Jake said some hip-hop artists like Biggie Small have taken Bob Marley's songs and cut them with their own music, and it works very well. I asked him why he hated pop music so much. He said it was all just commercial, sellout stuff.

My mom tried to warn him that he might be cutting himself off from some pleasures just because they are mainstream. My mom's comment really set Jake off for some reason. He yelled at her and told her to leave him alone. This had not happened in so long that my mom and I froze. She looked so hurt, damaged and scared.

I know he isn't using again, but he is trying to quit smoking. I think my mom worries and wonders if anything will ever be repaired. Maybe, maybe not. I wish my mom could love the maps of ancient Greece. It might make her happy to think and trace the coastline and to imagine a brightness that matters.

Tess ponders

No offense to Mia, but Jake and I had fun when we were kids and my dad was out of town visiting family. We ate out a lot because my mom found a really great place for macaroni and cheese. It was a kid-size meal, and it came with a homemade chocolate-chip cookie and milk. During those days, she hated to cook. She says now the kitchen never felt like it had anything to do with her. Not that she is a neat freak by any stretch of the imagination, but the mess was so firmly my father's: ethnic spices and fish oil. He was not good about cleaning up after himself, so the kitchen seemed to always smell exotic for sure—turmeric and coconut, cinnamon. It wasn't bad, even nice. Just odd—all that spilling and no cleaning up.

When my father was out of town, we were allowed to jump on his and my mother's bed.

And—this is the part I remember the best and love so much—she would let us stand on the dresser and jump to the bed and was always there to catch or help. My mom would also do these imitations like she was a mean monster, and she would say she was the only boss of the family, and then she would chase us, to the squeals and delight of both Jake and me. She had a wildness that was not there during her times with my father. And I think, maybe, it is good—that the wildness did not exist. I probably could not have kept up with her giant ways—giant in voice and, somehow, even her body.

When my father was home and my mother worked, my father would take me to the zoo. There was slowness to the days that I enjoyed. I loved the way he carried me on his shoulders or how we could stroll through the zoo. I was not really against my father, not until he moved out.

I guess some parents design activities to enhance their children's intelligence. But my parents were interested in self-survival. This actually had many benefits for us, Jake and me. My mother, when she was "parenting," was always devising ways for us to have attention that required quiet. She was available for cuddling and reading out loud or writing love notes with her finger on our backs. She says now that she was worried that if she danced or jumped the way she wanted to, it would stress my father. That is not true, I think. Or only partly. The real problem is that we could ignore my father in our jumpiness and physicalness.

My father's focus was food—everything from McDonald's to the Asian grocery store with its giant root plants and strange-looking fish. With him, it was not art or music classes but very memorable trips to the grocery store that sold pigs' feet in jar. In high school, I have gained some sort of cachet with my teachers because of the esoteric knowledge I have gained about food. Tomatoes are not from Italy but South America. Teachers are impressed, and other kids ask for my help on social-studies projects when they want to do a poster on the history of chocolate or something.

When my parents pulled us together and told us we were

going to reorganize the family—my father would be moving down the street—I was not distressed. I knew my mother's inclination would be to give in to our demands. In the past, she'd let us make recipes and let us have swear nights.

Homework, however, was always an issue. Jake's dyslexia meant that my mom was pretty involved with him. She would spend hours trying to find a place with no background noise or distractions—she was always trying to find new ways to help him not be discouraged and to stay focused on his assignments.

I was jealous, but one night she was able to take me away by myself. She took me to her office that had a conference room and a big flipchart. I was studying sentence structures, and we drew pictures of nouns and acted out the verbs. When we left, we stopped by a convenience store to buy a chocolate bar to celebrate, but she did something wrong and was pulled over by the police. I guess the police did not like her wide turns. My mom seemed so disappointed that this would be the end of our successful night together, and she tried to explain this to the cop. But the officer only seemed very concerned about her turn and then whether or not I had a seatbelt on. He flashed his flashlight brightly on me and scared me. My mom was getting irritated with him, and I did not know how she would handle this. When she is mad, all common sense goes out the window. He ran a search on my mom's driver's license and dismissed her, but our good cheer was gone. We drove in silence for a while.

I know my parents had some challenging times. It seemed like there were many deaths between my ninth and tenth birthdays: grandfathers on both sides, my mother's brother, my father's brother.

When my father wanted to go to Washington State for his brother's funeral, my mom said, "But you have not spoken to him in fifteen years, and we have no money." Forever after, my father would bring up this affront, and when he did, she would roll her eyes. It was around this time my mom took to hanging clothes up at night, which we thought so funny and strange.

Then the reorganization occurred. I am not sure why my mom called it that. She still loved my father? She actually believed a reorganization is different from a divorce? Out of something, guilt or longing on both their parts, it seems like we saw my father more after the reorganization. When we arrived home, he was always sitting on the porch. She would ignore him, and he would smoke cigarettes, something he had never done when we were not reorganized. She ignored him for as long as she could, but sometimes she invited him in. He would walk from room to room, always a shoulder bag on his shoulder. I could see him standing behind my mother, and then she would realize he was there and jump a little.

Should we have seen it coming, that my father would someday become delusional and grandiose? He went into the hospital for sadness and came back hyper and crazy. He would write these pretty graphic poems to my mother, and when we came home, they would be strewn across the yard.

There is now what has been etched in my mind as "the huge disaster"—when he tried to break into my aunt's house, the day my mom was fired. We were so confused, especially when he started to shout that he had secret information from God and he was going to take up the sword to make sure justice was done. My aunt pushed us, including my mom, into her room, locked the door; after two hours, we were told we could come out. My mom's brother and sister were there and explained that our father was on the way to get help.

One of the great things about my mother's closeness to her family is we do not need to feel embarrassed about anything. That night after my father was taken to the hospital, we tried to eat dinner. But when that didn't work, Aunt Debra pulled out a half-gallon of ice cream, and we spent the next hour passing chocolate-chip ice cream around, eating it with spoons and not talking. Mia, my mom and I slept together that night—it was the night that changed all nights.

My mom wants me to take a yoga or a Pilates class the way some of my friends do. I am not that interested. I stretch quite a bit and feel I have my own routine for strength and flexibility.

Though the other day, I spent the night with my mother's friend Angela. Angela has an amazing house. Angela runs, and while I was half-asleep, I heard her get up to run. It was her 5:00 a.m. run. After the run, her running partners came over and visited. They made me feel welcome, and I loved being wrapped in a bathrobe and eavesdropping. Angela announced that she had made my specialty in my honor: Swedish pancakes, coffee and eggs. We sat on the patio, and everyone laughed at me for being so Type A.

After the runners left, I was helping to clear the table, and I found myself crying. Angela asked what the matter was, and I said I didn't know but maybe it was because I had never seen anything so happy and relaxed as her breakfast table.

Angela took me by the shoulders and looked at me and

said, "The truth is I have been lucky. My friends and I sitting with our warm cup of coffee and the time and energy to have this type of morning."

I looked at her strangely; I did not believe her, and finally I told her so. "No," I said, "you did something right."

"No, Tess," Angela said, "because that would mean you did something wrong, which you did not. Nor did your mother or any of you. The world is random and not moral. I am not telling you this not because you are old enough to hear this but because you are smart enough to hear this."

Angela continued by saying the only difference between her and my mother is that "Joy doesn't have my intolerance; she is understanding."

I asked Angela, even though I felt like it could be a betrayal, why she liked my mother. She laughed. "We have been friends since Catholic high school. Joy took me away from myself because she was so different and interesting. She could cry at anything. Recently, she called crying because there was an invasion of ants in her house. I came over, and we took care of the problem by hosing down her outside wall and patio. I think I would love Joy even if we did not share a childhood—though our childhoods were different. Her family was known for being arty types and intellectuals. It was fun to go to her parents' house in college; it made you feel like you were part of something vital. There would be music, conversations about the end of the world. It was ludicrous, and it was exciting."

I felt so grown up hearing these things and like I was part of some majestic secret. I knew nothing about my mother's childhood. Only that she missed her mom more than her dad. She says it is because "my mom and I were not finished." I almost understood. If my mom died, it would feel so terrible for the simple reason that I am filled with a sense of something—what is it, security? When I say goodnight with the complete knowledge that in the morning I will say, "Good morning." What would happen if each night you went to bed, and you knew that each morning you would not say, "Good morning"?

Angela changed the subject. She told me that there is a marathon to prepare for; it is a fundraiser for NAMI, the National Institute for the Mentally Ill. Angela said, "I think your mother will appreciate that. When Frank was hospitalized, she would call NAMI every day, and they would instruct her on what questions to ask. She says with NAMI's coaching, she was able to extend Frank's hospitalization from two days to two weeks. So I will prepare for this marathon. I hope your mother does not cry and tell me how touched she is because that will drive me crazy."

My father has never come back to the house again. After his hospitalization, he did not come by even to visit. My mom cried and cleaned. She became, though, so fully our mom, with a firmness I have come to rely on. I am not sure I would ever change anything. So much has fallen away, my mom, brother and sister. We are bone and love to each other now. We are the strongest skeletons I know.

1986
Joy makes history, part 4

When I arrived, my siblings had gathered. Michael lived in town, and Jim and I arrived from out of town. Our father wore a dark-blue cardigan even though the weather was extremely warm for March. We hugged. Debra and her husband had cooked our mother's favorite meal, chicken paprikash, dumplings, salad and warm chocolate soufflé.

"This is exquisite, Debra," I said. "Thank you." Then, "Dad, what do you want? Do you want to sleep in the same room with her?" He did, but didn't think he would be strong enough if she needed anything during the evening. So we all slept in the room. We children lying on the floor in sleeping bags and tickling each other's back after our father was asleep and telling stories.

"Remember when my mom forgot to pick us up at the swimming pool?" or "Gosh, she was a bad cook."

"Remember there were two sets of nuns, those who hated her for being outspoken and the ones that secretly cheered her on."

I called Roxanne. I knew this was important. Roxanne thanked me for calling her and said she couldn't wait for me to come back, and we would have our dinners again. "Roxanne," I said, "I think I am in love." I told Roxanne about Frank. How he took care of me when I didn't even know I was dying.

"Well, if that boy has you well-fed and smiling and likes poetry, I am on his side." I was so appreciative of Roxanne's kindness and realized how much I had missed her. While taking a walk with Debra, I reported that I thought I was in love.

"How do you know?" she responded.

"How do I know? Because I let him be kind to me. I have never allowed that. I know I can give love, but for some reason, this time, I am letting myself be loved."

Debra asked if he was handsome. "Well, no. He is short, overweight and has the kindest eyes imaginable."

"Hmm," Debra responded. "Job?"

"No, he is a graduate student like me. Is there any way I can bring him in to meet Mom?"

"Joy, can't you be realistic for once?"

I called Frank daily and gave reports. My mother was slipping in and out of a coma. I was sitting with her and making sure she was hydrated. Frank suggested that I whisper to her as hearing was the last sense to go. I took Frank's advice and leaned over to my mother and told her about Frank. That I was loved and happy.

My mother rolled her eyes toward me and said, "Please, no ugly grandchildren." Those were her last words to me.

The following night, we four children and our father sat down for dinner, and we toasted our mother. Debra said there were some difficult logistics to work out. Of course, our father, Dan, would live with Debra and her husband, Robert. But Debra had just gotten a new job and would be required to work evenings and even be out of town. Michael couldn't help, even though he was in town, because he had children. We had promised our mother we would take good care of Dan and make sure he was not lonely.

"Joy," Debra said, "we need to ask you to make the largest sacrifice, but that is because you have the most flexible life right now. Move back to Tucson. You can take up your studies here. Help us, help your father. We have helped you so long."

I burst into tears. Debra was right. It was time for me to be helpful. I felt like I could give up Seattle and even transport my graduate studies. But Frank? Roxanne? People who made me feel at home in my own skin. I felt silly. Frank and I had been together for so little time. But not touching him daily, the thought of that made my skin hurt.

My mother died that evening. When they arrived from the funeral home, I was adamant that my father not see her body be taken away. I went to the chair where my father sat, walked him into the spare bedroom and stood by the door.

"Are they gone?" I yelled at Debra.

"Yes" was the response.

"The coast is clear, Daddy," I said. He came out, and we all said a rosary for her—no, not for her; it was for our father. My mother would have hated the ritual.

It was an Irish wake. Singing and drinking. Immediately afterward, Debra moved into the house our father had shared with our mother.

I was too frightened to explain to Frank any of Debra's pleas, so I simply asked him to meet me at his apartment on the night of my arrival. Roxanne picked me up, and I explained that I would be leaving the Northwest and returning to the hot desert. Roxanne was supportive. "I can't wait to visit," she said.

I brought Roxanne to meet Frank. I wished Frank had straightened up the apartment for us. Roxanne didn't seem to mind. We ate stir-fry vegetables with hot bean sauce and mango chutney. I watched as Roxanne's eyes and mouth feasted on Frank's cooking.

She left, and Frank and I made love. I started to weep, and he encouraged me. He wept too; he could only imagine my sadness.

I told him my sister's plea. I was not to worry, Frank assured me. He would follow me in a few short months when he was finished with graduate school. Frank went with me to the department chair. Stood by me as I told him that I regretted that I could not use the scholarship money. He wished me well. Professor Dolan said, "We will miss you. I know Mark, especially, will. I will let him know when he returns from his sabbatical. "

Because I did not know what to say, I said, "Thank you."

Mia looks out the window

I promised my mom I would not get in the car with my father because he took lots of medicine, and she was afraid he would not be the best driver. But I did once get in the car with him. Jake was there and Tess too. So we all did. We all broke this rule my mom had made up, and it was a very serious rule in the sense that she had a family meeting to announce it. Those were rare, family meetings, so we did tend to pay attention.

She called us together and said, "Your father is a very fine person, and no one is allowed to speak poorly of him. Do you understand?" She looked at each of us. We nodded. "However, I need each of you to promise that you will not get in a car with him." My father had left the halfway house for the mentally ill and gotten his own apartment. When he was in the halfway house, none of us was quite sure how he could spin to our house a few times a week, each time with a different car, though all of them were versions of minivans he used to drive us around in when we were children. Finally, he explained that he bartered cooking with the other residents for use of the car.

However, after a few weeks of my father arriving at all times of the day, I once looked out the window, and there was my mother standing in the driveway with her arms across her chest. And she was saying to my father, who looked a little confused, "Frank, you are a great person, but you may not come to this house like this anymore. You can call, and we will meet you at a park."

My father said, simply, "OK."

I was so relieved there was not a scene or anything that might happen in a book. I believe I had my share of scenes with my father, and I just didn't want them anymore. Like, the quota of weirdness from my family had been met. With my mom losing her job, Jake and drugs, and my father, it was enough. I was scared my mom might be thinking it was OK for more weirdness, and that was why she was out there. I consider it a lucky moment that he simply said, "OK." And things almost got normal, at least normal for us, when he was able to move into his own apartment, and we started meeting at a park every once in a while. At first, he had no car. He took the bus to meet us, but eventually he was able to get his own van.

My betrayal occurred right after I had finished reading *Harry Potter and the Deathly Hallows,* and I was very upset. I was very upset for several reasons. It was the last book in the series, and so that whole Harry Potter experience was now going to be gone: sneaking the book under my covers or locking myself in my mother's bathroom to read in her empty bathtub. I was upset also because Fred Weasley died. I couldn't believe it. The nicest person in the whole book just killed off. I was pretty devastated and snuck into my mother's room. She was out for the afternoon. I threw myself across my mother's bed and was really crying it up. I thought I had done a pretty good job of being discreet and sneaky about where I was, so when Tess knocked on the door and said, "Are you OK?" I was so surprised, I screamed.

"Whoa," she said. I felt so caught. And Tess would never understand how I could become so distraught from a book. She is always thinking so much about her own life, the concreteness of it, and the next steps of that life. She has always been a little impatient with the whole book thing. She did not even ask why I was crying. She just lay down with me on the bed and hugged me and started crying herself.

Then, after a few minutes, we started that laugh/crying thing. "Why are you crying?" I asked, and she said, "Oh, I don't know. Because I hate my bedroom. I hate that the furniture is so small. And there is no one I can tell because Mom would just roll her eyes. Why are you crying?" And I told her how Fred Weasley had died, and he was the nicest character. And he died fighting evil and trying to defend his family and Harry Potter, and it just killed me. Then we laughed/cried some more. And then there was a knock on the door again, and it was Jake, and we both screamed.

"What is going on in here?" he said, opening the door. Then he looked at us and said, "Oh, never mind."

Then he described the problem at hand. He was craving something with salt, like potato chips. And when he said that, Tess and I looked at each other and suddenly realized we were too. We were craving something with salt. But, of course, there was no money, and also how were we going to get to the corner store, but we really did need potato chips. I said, "First things first . . . we need the money. Here's what we do. Focus on the furniture. Loose change is going to fall behind the cushions and stuff. Jake, you take the living room, Tess and I will take the bedrooms." After about ten minutes, we gathered up about $2.39—a start but not enough for a large bag of potato chips.

It was when we were trying to figure out what to do next that we saw our father drive up. We knew that my mom did not want him in the house. In silent unison, we walked outside the house.

"Hey, Frank," said Jake.

Tess and I said, "Hi, Dad. What's going on?" But at the same moment we asked, we realized we really didn't want to know. So we didn't wait for an answer.

What Jake said was, "Hey, Frank, we have a problem. We want potato chips, but we are about a dollar fifty short. We found all the change there could possibly be underneath the seat cushions. Can you help us out?"

My dad looked confused. I said, "Hey, can we look through your car for loose change?"

"Well, it is not really my car. But sure." The car, owned by one of his housemates, was kind of a white minivan. It was squarer-looking. It had very stiff seats. Not like the minivans where you could easily move the seats forward and back. It was Tess who slipped her long arm between the seat cushions in the front passenger seat and pulled out a five-dollar bill.

We all looked at it like we had just found the Holy Grail. We didn't discuss whether or not it was OK to spend, nor did we skip a beat when my father said, "Get in the car. Let's go get those potato chips, and I guess I will buy one of those single cigarettes they sell."

We just did—we piled in, got a jumbo bag and even a Coke and went home. We ate them on the front porch. My father stood several feet away and smoked a cigarette, just watching us. I didn't mind him being there. I asked him what he was cooking these days. He said he was trying to doctor up some frozen fish sticks that were in the freezer.

"How do you do that?" I asked.

He said, "It has to be in the sauce, the tartar sauce. I throw in some chili and lime, and that helps."

We nodded and then looked down the street and saw my mother coming. It was then we all realized that we had broken her rule about getting in the car with my father.

"Oh, shit," said Jake.

Tess was the one who said, "If it comes up, about the car, we are going to have to lie." We all nodded.

My mom got out of the car with a small bag of groceries. "Hello, Frank," she said. "It would be better if we all met at the park, but thank you for not going in the house. I assume that was the case?"

"Yes, Joy," he said and then, "I will go now."

We all said goodbye, and that was it. It was never mentioned. My mom didn't ask if we drove with our father, and so we were spared the lie. She didn't notice the bag of potato chips that we had devoured. Jake walked to the house next door and threw the bag in the neighbor's garbage can that was waiting to be picked up.

I don't think I had ever betrayed my mom before this incident. It was unusual. It was unusual in that it was so easy. It was strange how bad I felt. Later that afternoon, I went into my mother's room. She was lying on her bed, kind of staring. She smiled and said, "Do you want to have a girl moment?" And I nodded yes and lay down beside her. Jake and Tess were gone someplace with my aunt Debra, and I was happy to have my mother to myself.

It was a Friday, but that didn't matter much now that my mom had lost her job. Friday was no longer special like it used to be, when we could go to a restaurant for dinner and take a walk and people-watch around the university, where my mom worked. It was a little before dinner, whatever that was going to be. The satisfaction of the potato chips was long gone.

"Mom," I said, "I know we are having a hard time, but I miss our adventures. Can we do something different?"

"Hmm," she said, "I hate using gas." I started to cry. I didn't mean to. I didn't want her to feel guilty or anything. I just felt so sad. She bolted out of bed and said, "Of course we are going on an adventure." She took ten dollars, and we stopped at the store and bought a chocolate bar, coffee for her, sour gummy worms for me, and we started to drive.

I was pretty scared about this adventure backfiring. That my mom would use it as an opportunity to "talk." Ask me how I was doing while trying to be casual.

But that didn't happen. It was just going to be a day of things not being the way I expected it to. She didn't say anything. And when I put in the CD I bought to play in the car, Little Joy, she said, "Can you turn that louder?" It is hard to describe the music of Little Joy because there is something plaintive about the lyrics, but also, at the same time, the tempo is upbeat. What I like is the lyrics are not strictly about romance. They could be taken in different ways. They could be about someone trying to make things better by leaving or just accepting that they are lonely. It is the certainty and acceptance of how they play their instruments and songs that is so appealing.

I didn't want to have to say any of this to my mom. And

it didn't look like she was going to ask me. I didn't ask where we were going. I thought I had really crossed a border by crying and letting her know about it, because she has so much going on. So I decided if she was going to make me talk about "stuff," I was going to do the best I can and try to. But she was just driving. She looked kind of pretty. I mean, she wasn't trying to hide that she had been crying, and so that meant she hadn't been crying. She said simply, "I have heard about this concept of driving aimlessly. It is supposedly good for thinking, for sorting things out. I think I get that a little. It is just that I am not the most relaxed person, and I don't want to use my air conditioner."

We drove into the foothills. My mom laughed and said, "This is where people like to come and kiss their sweethearts. It is beautiful, but I promise I won't try to kiss you." And it was beautiful: the sun was setting, and the car was parked right against the mountains. My mom stayed in the car, but I took a blanket and spread it on the hood of the car. Little Joy was playing. They have this female singer, and she just has this unusual voice. Definitely sad but so accepting that you can't help but feel hopeful—like anything can happen, and you can live with it and even make some dignified song out of it.

I started thinking about Fred Weasley from the Harry Potter books and that the saddest thing is how sad those who keep living are. And how I don't really believe you get united with anyone after you die. I mean, how would that work? Like there is a dead hotel filled with people waiting to be united with those still on earth and still alive. And you go and wait by the elevator to greet loved ones as they exit the living floor and enter the dead floor. It didn't make any sense to me. But all those people here on earth. That was who I felt sorry for—my mom, my dad, still trying to piece it together while those they loved, their parents, my uncle Jim, they were just gone. I don't believe they were waiting for any of us. And that made me kind of sad, but what was I supposed to do? I couldn't suddenly believe in a bunch of lonely saints waiting for me to be in their club.

I think my mom and I stayed there a pretty long time. All through the Little Joy CD and through this Leonard Cohen tribute called *I Am Your Man*. It was nearly dark when she stuck her head out the window and said, "Are you ready?" I nodded my head. I guess I was ready, or maybe I was never going to be ready, and maybe they amount to the same thing. What I mean is we are always waiting, aren't we? To hear good news or bad news. To see if my father's medicine was going to work this time.

I think it was my mother not asking me any questions and just letting me listen to the music that made me want to claim this evening as one of the most perfect of my dozen-year life, though I was getting to be very close to thirteen. I said so to my mother. "This was pretty perfect. Thank you." And as if to somehow be possessed by something magnificent, she just grabbed my hand, squeezed and smiled. No questions. I asked her, even though I had already asked for so much, if we could go the long way around to the house. I just wanted to look out the window at the houses and streetlights and imagine nice things happening to families. Not like winning the lottery or anything. But, let's say, a family playing Parcheesi or cards.

When we got home, Jake and Tess were there, back from hanging out with my aunt Debra. I had a vague notion for a moment that I would ask anyone if they wanted to play a board game. We had a few board games, but I was too competitive, and Jake was easily frustrated and my mom and Tess easily bored. So I decided against it.

Besides, Jake and Tess were in a huge fight. What I gather is that it was about a mutual friend or a mutual ex-friend that Jake had ditched. Tess thought this put her in a precarious position with this person. Overall, Tess was pretty unhappy with the way things were going for Jake in the friend department. She was happy he was sober and everything, but he had drifted away from the friends that he did drugs with. In her heart, Tess knew that was a good thing. But, on the other hand, these people at least said hi to her. Not so with these new friends, these hipster people who were coming over and talking music and different artists and drawing together. It unnerved Tess. Tess preferred hip-hop alienation songs; Jake liked those, too, but not exclusively.

From what I gathered from the argument, Tess was upset that he was now with people who were too familiar with life being comfortable; she didn't think any of them had suffered like us or even his drug friends. This is what my mom and I caught as we came in the door. "Huh?" said my mother.

Then Tess explained her point to my mom: "Jake's new friends are all just middle-class people; they would never understand the lyrics of a Tupac song."

Why my mother knew about Tupac, I will never know. Anyway, my mom said, "You do? You understand the lyrics of a Tupac song? You know about violence and despair and racism?" She seemed a little agitated, my mother. "Because let me make clear one thing: You don't. We don't. But you know what you do have in common with Tupac?" she asked, doing that squinty-look thing she does. We all looked at her. "Tupac loved his mother very much. He adored his mother. Let the adoration begin." She smiled, pointing at herself.

Tess was annoyed that her stream of screaming had been interrupted but was thrown off guard too. Jake told Tess to shut the fuck up. That she didn't know what she was talking about. He owed her nothing but especially not friends. And if he thought that he would still hang out with friends just because Tess thought they were cool, then she was nuts. He was using a very mean voice, and it scared me. Tess started crying and went to her room and slammed the door.

I felt bad for her, I really did. Sometimes I even worried about Tess more than Jake. And I didn't even know that was possible. I didn't worry about drugs, but what would happen to her? This very pretty girl who thinks she is ugly. This very smart girl who thinks she is dumb. This very lonely girl who does not like to read books. What kind of refuge is possible for her?

I took from my closet my secret stash of savings. My aunt Debra had helped me start it. I promised it would only be used for emergencies and that I would discuss those emergencies with her. I didn't even think about it earlier in the day when we had our potato-chip crisis. I took $3.50; this was my second betrayal of the day. The first, of course, was getting in the car with my father. I tapped on Tess's door, and she was mean about that. The way she said, "What do you want?"

I persevered. "I found some change. Do you want to go for a walk, and maybe I can get you a candy bar or something?"

She gave me a mean look. But still, I persevered. And tried to communicate "come on" with my expression. So she got off her bed and started looking for her shoes. And while she looked for them, I had to try to sell another outing, this time with Tess, to my mother.

She was in her room, trying to read and looking up job openings on the computer. I said casually, "Tess and I are going for a walk."

Without looking up, she said, "But it is dark outside."

"I know, Mom, but we need a little walking, a little exercise." I knew she was not going to be able to argue with that.

She looked at me like she was trying to think about what I said but the words were having a hard time penetrating. She is like that when she is distracted. I knew her distraction would work to my advantage. "No farther than the park, and do not go into the park. Do you understand?"

"Deal," I replied.

Tess and I stopped by the corner store, and I bought her a Reese's candy bar. When she asked where I got the money, I just shrugged my shoulders. I felt like I had met my quota of untruths for the day, with getting in my father's car and taking money without discussing it with my aunt Debra. She accepted my shrug as a good enough answer and did not ask for details. It must have been my lucky day because Tess let that go.

She went on and on about Jake and his new friends. That they were milquetoasts, and, with Jake's history, he needed people "who had seen shit, like me, like us." I didn't disagree with that statement. She had seen shit; we all had. But I didn't know how she knew what other people had seen or not seen.

I was getting worried because she was getting pretty upset, and there was something wrong about her claim. It bothered me. I hate to say it, I was afraid it lacked generosity. What did she know about other people's "personal geography"? I had heard my mother use that phrase once.

"Tess, let's talk about something different just for a moment," I proposed. Then she started in on how I was younger than she was, and I had no idea what she was going through, and I had no business telling her what to do. I was just about to give up. I had pretty much had it. I knew what she was proposing with this diatribe, that she should be loved enough, so much so that someone could make *it* stop. *It* being her talk to herself. "Tess," I said, as if the conversation were happening between us and not just in my head and separately in her own head. "It is not going to work this way. OK? You have to do all the hard work. The hard, hard work of changing the way things are. I know it is not fair. But only you can do that."

She said, "That is bullshit. My mom needs to come here right now and make things better. She brought us into this fucking world."

I don't know why, but I slapped her and started to run away. She ran after me, and we started to fight, right there in public. I was mortified, and I could not stop.

This lady walked out of her house and said, "Hey, hey, what is going on?" We tried to say we were only kidding. But she asked, "Where is your mother?" We told her she was at home. To our despair, she said, "Take me to her." And so we did, in perfect silence. When we got home, the lady knocked on the door, and my mom answered. The lady told my mom what she saw. She seemed to imply it was my mother's fault. That she had clearly let things get out of hand. If I wasn't so ashamed and embarrassed, I might have apologized.

But, instead, I sat at the dining room table. Tess tried to go into her room. But my mom said, "Get out here." Tess tried to ignore her. Then my mother did something shocking: she pulled Tess's hair and told her to go sit at the table. Tess did. Tess must have been in shock because she was very compliant. My mother sat across from us with hands folded. She did not say a word; she just stared at us with the scary look. I think it was a full five minutes, maybe even ten, of silence. Then she said, "I want you both to go to your room for the rest of the night. Go," she said. And we did. We each got up and went to our rooms.

Tess started to wail the moment she got into her room. My mother stood outside her door and said, "Stop it. If you continue to cry, you will be on restriction for the next month."

What kind of ultimatum is that: "If you cry, you are on restriction for the next month"? Had my mother lost it? Of course she had, I knew. She had lost it. But hadn't we all? Jake, Tess and me? We had lost something. It wasn't exactly normalcy, but that might be close. I couldn't stand thinking this way.

This focus on less. It was pessimistic. It was close to the way Tess felt. So I tried to think about what we had gained. If you lose, then you also have to gain.

We had gained the ability to read faces, like my mom's face. To use it to understand her moods and how they might manifest themselves to us. My brother and sister and I gained the ability to look for loose change together and to tell lies together. We had gained each other, whether we wanted to or not. I knew that Jake would try to tickle my back if I needed it. Tess, I know, would do the laugh/cry thing with me. We had gained the night, with its loose affiliation of planets and light. We had gained the placeless wind.

I got out of my bed, put in my Little Joy CD, turned off the light and went to sleep.

Tess attempts to clear up some things

I just came out and asked my mother, "Did you mean to have children?"

She said, "Yes."

And then I said, "Are you happy that you had children?"
She said, "Yes."

And then I said, "Is there anything else you would like to say?"

She said, "No." And then, after a pause, "Well, having children is much harder than I imagined."

That annoys me to no end. What kind of consumer is that? Didn't she do any homework on the matter of having children? And what does she mean by "harder"? She means me, doesn't she? She means me. I can tell by the way she says it. Me. The middle one. The one who is always dissatisfied, and she has said this when she was really mad. She said, "For God's sake, why are you always so dissatisfied?" And then, and I will never forget this, "Get over yourself." And she said it in a kind of mean voice, and to this day she has not apologized for saying that. Can you imagine saying that to your daughter?

Unbelievable.

But where can I go? And what can I do? It is not like other divorces, where I can go live with my father. That option is not possible. That fact might have crossed her mind if she had done some homework into the matter. She could have thought about the possible scenarios when she was thinking up the idea to have a family. Clearly, she had not considered our situation—divorce, where no option is possible for alternative living arrangements.

At first, I didn't want to have anything to do with my father after the disaster. After he tried to break down the door and tell my mom about talking to God. I had never seen the expression on my mother's face, never on her or on anyone else. Let me try to explain it. It was almost animal-like. An animal in total fear. Like I had seen on the Wild Life channel. Like, "How am I going to put these babes in my mouth and run away?" But she didn't run away. We didn't.

Still, couldn't it have crossed her mind that this could happen? Back in the day when she and Frank were all dewy-eyed in love? That it might happen? I can hear my uncle Mike saying, "Yeah, that sucks; let's move on." For just one moment, I would like to not move on. Everyone is telling me to get over it, as if it were the flu. My profound sense is that this is unjust; people treat my situation like it is just a spell. Something I just need to shake off. I don't think that is fair.

After he got out of the psychiatric hospital, and after Jake got out of rehab, I would see my father around town. It was embarrassing. I should have felt sorry for him or worried, but I wasn't. He hung out in this section of town where hipsters go. He would be walking and bumming cigarettes, and

I would see him where I waited for my bus or ate pizza with friends after school. I would hide. Go into the bathroom and just wait. My friends thought he was cool. That it was cool to have a dad who didn't nag you about your grades or washing the car, stuff like that.

I hate to say this, but I was mad because I missed him, and he scared me. When I was young, he said everyone, even the grocery clerk, would make the observation that there was a special bond between us. He took me everywhere. He would bring Jake to a babysitter, but me he would toss up on his shoulders and bounce around. I loved being up high on his shoulders. At the grocery store, I could see the rows and rows of shelves, like a sea of things, and it was exciting to see it as a whole and then try to break it down. At first, all you see are boxes and cans, but the trick is, the fun thing was, to try to distinguish the boxes. Figure out which rows are the macaroni boxes and which are the graham-cracker boxes. I wanted to see that difference.

Unfortunately, though, anyone who has a parent who is mentally ill has to ask: Is this possible for me? But I feel I have to ask it more deeply and longer than Jake or Mia because of this bond I have with my father.

I explained this to my mother's friend Angela. She is the only one I felt I could discuss this with. I need someone who was not blood. Angela said that the good things, the trips to the zoo, the library and the songs my father and I made up together, they are real and count. That those good things exist with my father's mental illness or no mental illness. She wants me to call it *mental illness* and not *crazy*. But, Dad, my pop, he says the word *crazy*.

I appreciated this thought. Actually, there were two

thoughts Angela gave me. One was helping me see that the fun things I did with my father were still fun and important. I like to think about that.

Let's say, when I am trying to get this stupid hair of mine straight or am experimenting with makeup, I think of the fun memories with my dad. Angela even said, "Revel in the good times you had with your dad."

The other thought, the reason she wants me to call it *mental illness*, is to make me try to think of it like, well, an illness. Once she said, "You wouldn't be mad at your father if he had cancer or diabetes.

You would just make sure he got the best medical attention possible. Mental illness is like that. Just another thing that forces you to go to the doctor."

"But what about me?" I asked. "I could possibly catch this thing, isn't that so?"

"Well, it is equally possible, maybe even a better chance, that you won't get it." Then she asked, "You hate uncertainty, don't you?" I had to admit that was true. So she said, "Well, let's make a list of all the things we are certain about: I love you, your mother loves you, and your father loves you. Those are things that are certain and will not change."

What if my mother decides, though, she doesn't love me? That could be possible and true for all sorts of reasons. I can be extremely rude, for instance. Sometimes, I can see it in my head. I can hear it. I can imagine it. When my mom says, "How was school?" I know what she is really saying is, "What the fuck, why are you getting a D in math?" And even though she is not saying that, I feel I must respond. So I might say, "You are so rude. Why don't you come out and say, 'You are my dumb kid'?" And, depending on what kind of day my mom has had, we are off and yelling at each other for hours, or she is locked behind her bedroom door. I can see her in there, staring out the window, worried, fidgeting with her fingers and hands. It makes me so mad. Why can't she see that I need her at that moment? How can she be so blind?

For a while, my father was in a halfway house, and then he got permission to move out and be on his own as long as he stayed in touch with his caseworker and did not randomly come to our house. I think my mother complained to someone, and that became a condition of his being able to move out of the halfway house. It was when he was living on his own that I decided to just call him, and I did. And I said, "I just want you to know that I forgive you for the time you ran to the house and started screaming about talking to God. And maybe saying Mom should die or something like that."

And he said, "Tess, I thank you for that. And I am proud of you for saying that." Those words melted my heart. I felt like it had been so long since someone had said, "I am proud of you."

Then I did this thing my mom told me to do once, which is always ask the other person questions. It makes them feel better. So I asked him about when I was born, and what did he remember? He said he rewrote this old political song and sang it to my mom while she was nursing me. He said the original words were "I am sticking to the union, sticking to the union, till the day I die." He switched them to "I am sticking to the Tess girl, the Tess girl, till the day I die." Then he said, "And I will, Tess."

Then he told me that right after I was born, his own mother died, and he had been with her. That she was rest-

204

less and in pain. And he just stared at her, and she stared at him. And one of his brothers said, "Why are you two talking so privately with your eyes?" He said he was able to tell his mother that it was OK to die, and she did.

I told him about fighting with my mom and that I was really mad at her. That she was mean and was always dissatisfied with everything—my grades, my attitude and my room. He told me something that I had never known before. He said my mom's mom was mean and said some unkind things to my mother. And that he wished my mother could remember that better. I asked if my grandmother liked him. He laughed and said, "Oh, no. She thought your mother should marry a professor or a lawyer."

And I said, "Did that bother you?"

My father replied, "I had the last laugh, don't you think? I know and knew Joy better than her own mom. Who can say that? Not many people. I knew every sadness but also every meal and every dessert she loves. Those are things a mother should know, but Joy's mother didn't. I did."

I began to wonder if meanness was genetic. My grandmother, my mother and now me. That kind of scared me as much as the mental illness scared me. I was and am still so angry with my mother. I blame her completely for this mess I am in. The mess I am in is dissatisfaction. And I want to punch anyone who says to just get over it. And what if that is my nature, something I cannot get over? I tried to bring this up with my mother quite a few times, but it only ended up in a fight.

But just the other day, she was doing the dishes, and no one else was at home. I went up to her, and in a very calm voice, I said, "Remember I asked you about did you want to have children? And you said yes but it was more difficult than you thought? Well, I would like to ask you what you meant by that."

"By what?" she asked.

And I had to practice my yoga breathing, something I learned in class. I can take yoga for PE, and we learned this calming way to breathe, which is you try to concentrate on seeing your breath come in and out of the nostrils. I did that, and I said, "What did you mean by *difficult*?"

"Oh," she said and wiped her hands on the towel. She sat down at the crammed table in the kitchen and said, "Well, I thought I could just love you with all of my heart, and it would be good. But it isn't good enough, is it? When you were little, you were scared of swimming, and at first I was mad because I thought, Why can't she feel safe? She knows I am here. I love her; why doesn't she feel safe? And I had to think about it. And maybe there were ten thousand reasons you didn't feel safe. Maybe it had to do with your body temperature. Maybe you had a bad experience once while I was washing you. Maybe your brother teased you around water. And maybe that was why you were afraid of water. And I could not love any of that away. I wish I could love all these difficult things away."

I looked at her. I was surprised at this. I thought she was going to tell me it was difficult because she couldn't go out, or she gave up swimming laps because of me—something like that. She looked sad. I hate it when she looks sad. And I said, "But you are still happy, right, that you had children?"

"Of course," she said.

"With Frank?" I asked.

"Who else?" she replied.

And I said, "I dunno, there could have been others—an English professor?"

My mom looked startled. "Why would you say that?" she asked.

"Maybe it would have made your mom happier?"

"Ah," she said, "the old let's-make-Mom-happy syndrome. I swear to you, Tess, you are forbidden to think it is your job to make me happy. It is your job to make Tess happy. In spite of your mother, your father or anyone else. It is the hardest assignment imaginable, but you must make it so. Do you understand?"

This whole conversation was getting stranger by the minute. I didn't expect this at all. I was hearing for the first time that my mom was freaked out because she didn't know why I was scared of water, and in addition to that, she was giving me an assignment to not make her happy. What was I supposed to do with this? "Mom," I said, "what if I want to make you happy?"

Then she got that look again; it was almost the same as when my dad tried to come into the house and was yelling about God. But what she did was she started pounding her fist on the table. "Don't, don't, don't! You are not allowed to care about that. Do you understand?"

But I persevered. "Why?" I asked.

And she said, "Because it will not work."

"You mean you will never be happy?"

"I don't think I mean that, Tess."

"What do you mean? Does this have anything to do with my father?"

"No, I don't think so, Tess. It just has to do with it not being possible. Because I am, in many ways, just an invention, someone you made up. If you tried to make me happy, it wouldn't work because the mom that is in your brain doesn't really exist."

That scared and puzzled me, and she could see that. "It is like the time we went to that movie. Let's see, was it *Notting Hill*?" And for you it was a movie about cute clothes, and for me it was a movie about a bookstore. And who knows what other type of movie it was even for the people who starred in it."

This is when my mom can make me super angry. "Are you equating being a mom with being in a movie?"

"Sort of," she said.

And I just came right out and said it: "That is rude and irresponsible." I said, "How would you like it if your very mom told you your life with her is a movie? That your life together was the equivalent to about two hours, and if the stars are in alignment, then you get popcorn? And what if your mom told you that is what it is about? That her mom-ness really is a two-hour stint with or without popcorn?"

"But that might be a good thing, Tess. Because you get to be in charge of the movie that you see, and, hopefully, your mom was a good mom, and she gets to be in your movie again and again. And in your movie, the one you are starring in, the people are interesting, and they don't hurt you, ever, at all."

"How possible is that?" I said sarcastically.

And she said, "Not very possible."

Then I was furious with her again. "What are you trying to say? That you are miserable? That happiness is not pos-sible?" She was beginning to look tired. I knew I needed to try to tone it down, but I wasn't sure I could; she gets me so upset. She is like the water I supposedly hated as a child. I just could not get a handle on her. I could not get anything solid from her, ever.

"Listen, Tess, I have upset you, right?"

And I just said, "I would like you to justify that you think our life together is a movie that will not last."

"Justify?" my mother asked. "What do you mean by that?" she wanted to know.

I said, "How can that be all right? How can me being in your life being the equivalent of two hours be all right?"

"I didn't say it was all right, Tess. I just said . . . " Then she trailed off and said simply, "I love you and want you to be happy."

This is how so many of our conversations ended, with my mom defeated and me, well, dissatisfied. I said, "I think we are through for now." And I walked out the front door. I slammed the front door.

My mom came outside and said, "Where are you going? And do not slam this door. Come back and apologize right now."

But I just shouted over my shoulder, "I am going for a walk."

And I did. I walked to the park near the house. It took a while for things to quit being a blur. Part of me didn't even understand what my mom was saying. This philosophy shit she goes into, it might work for Jake or Mia but not me. I want real things. I want a real mom, and why can't she get that?

But inside my brain and body, I could hear myself

scream: What is a real mom? Not Joy. Joy is not a real mom.
She wants to be a cloud floating through the sky. I basically
heard her say that. Here for a moment and then gone.

As if I didn't have enough already taken away. I was special to my dad, and I mattered. Now what? What does that
mean or matter? Ugh. I wanted out—I wanted out of my
brain. Out of the corner of my eye, I saw this homeless guy.
This one that my mom and Jake seemed fascinated by. The
one near the church my mom goes to. Once we were all in
the car, and we drove by the church, and both my mom and
Jake said at the same time, "There's Ted." They both looked at
him but in a strange way. They looked at him like they both
knew him, but he was a different person to each of them.

He was trying to get water. But the faucet was too hard to
turn. I went over, and I said, "Let me turn this on for you. It
is hard to turn." I told him with a laugh, "You need two hands
to turn the faucet, making drinking the water impossible.
Let me get it for you."

He nodded his head just a little—in appreciation, I
think. He scooped his head down and drank. Then he
looked at me and said, barely audibly, "Can you keep holding it, just a little longer?" I shook my head as if to say, "Of
course."

He cupped his hands and waited till they filled with
water, and he splashed that on his face. He did that about six
times. And as he did it, a slight smile came across his face.
"Delicious," I think he muttered. Then he took out several
plastic bottles and began to fill them up.

After about the third bottle, I said, "My hands need a
break." He looked at me like he had forgotten I was there.
Like he thought the water was just being made available to

him on his own, without my assistance at all. And he nodded again in agreement that he understood it was time for
me to take a break. So I relaxed my hand from the faucet handle and shook it. Then I returned it to the handle.

He continued to fill his water bottles. It got so that he
would look at me and give a slight nod of appreciation.
When all of them were filled, he actually gave me a little bow.
And I bowed to him. I don't know why. I think I liked that
I was able to forget my anger for a moment. Forget Joy and
all her mumbo jumbo and to do something real. I helped
someone who needed water get water. And you know what I
liked the best? That we did not talk, barely at all. But still we
understood each other. I liked that I was of use. I liked that
he nodded as if to say I was on the right track. I liked that he
understood me when I said I needed a break, and he gave
me one. I liked that so much.

I began to walk home. But you know what? I really didn't
want to go home. I didn't need that right now, so I walked,
and I walked. All the way to the church my mom goes to and
where she first came across this homeless Ted. I didn't go
in the church. That would have been dramatic. But I walked
around it. The front, the side and the back. It had low windows, basement windows, and the glass was mottled. I ran
my fingers across the windows. I liked the way they were
bumpy, but when I looked at my fingers, they were dirty. I
guess you couldn't see it; you could only know it by touching, but the windows were dirty. That surprised me a little,
but I wiped my fingers on my pants and carried on.

I walked around that building about seven times. For the
first three times, I thought about my mom and dad. But I
tried to stop my thinking about them and our situation, to

breathe, like my yoga instructor says. "To focus on what you can actually change," she says in a kind of dramatic whisper. "Which is really where you put your right hand or your left, or how you lean. And if you get your right hand in the right place, the world will be right where you want it." That is what she says almost every yoga class.

Then I thought about Mia and Jake. There is this photograph of us together when we were kids. My arm was in a cast. When we looked at it recently, now grown up, I asked, "Jake, what were you thinking during this photograph?"

And he said, "I had just seen a snake, and I didn't want to tell anyone because I thought we would have to go home if I did."

"What about you, Mia?" I continued.

She said, "I have no idea, Tess. Look at me. I must have been one year old. What about you? What were you thinking?"

"I was thinking about my cast. How I had asked for a pink one, but they gave me a purple one. And I was wondering if pink and purple were the same color."

That cracked us up somehow. And ever since that day, Jake will randomly say, "Are pink and purple the same color?" And we will start laughing. It is a secret joke that my parents are excluded from. And that is sort of thrilling.

I wasn't so angry anymore, but I still did not want to go home. I walked to the park, and there he was again, Ted. But my mom was there too. She had obviously come looking for me. She was standing next to Ted; they were not talking. I could tell she was upset, that I had been gone too long. She just stood there looking and looking. When she saw me, she gave me a stern nod of her head to say, "Go home." She turned around and started walking home. I followed her, several feet behind her. I didn't really want to walk with her. I didn't. I wanted to be alone and on my own. I wanted to be all right. I wanted everyone to be all right. I looked up, and my mother was waiting for me at the corner. When I got there, she put her arm around me, and we walked home together. And not one word was said.

Jake discovers
the painter Miro

Joy would call it the ice-cream-and-bookstore trajectory. That was what she would do—throw in a fancy word, like *trajectory*, to try to make it seem less mundane. But in truth, she didn't need to do that. Even when I was a kid, I liked that particular trip, the ice-cream-and-bookstore trip, because I could get any flavor I wanted, and the bookstore didn't mind if we ate inside their store. And the bookstore smelled musty, and the bookshelves were so high. But I really loved this trip after I got out of rehab. I probably really needed the sugar, and the cold of the ice cream was great. And on the first trip after rehab, I discovered Joan Miro. He is this Spanish guy, a painter and a surrealist. A political person without being political. You know, never held office or anything, but he said some things, he said contradictory things at the same time and made them both be true. That was why I loved him. I am like that. I can feel two things, exactly the opposite, but at the same time believe them to both be true.

During the Spanish Civil War, he painted "Still Life with Old Shoe." What I learned, because I had my girlfriend read to me about him, is that this painting got him in a lot of trouble. It was an old shoe, a moldy piece of bread, an apple with a fork in it, a bottle of alcohol. I guess his surrealist friends got mad at him because he had drawn something sort of representational. But, really, he was just making a comment on his country, Spain, how everything normal, an apple, a shoe, had become tinged with regret and grayness. So this attitude, that Spain during its civil war had become a sallow place, got him in trouble with those in Spain. So he was lost. He was very sad, but he continued to paint, and he lived a long time.

Now, I am not going to compare myself to Miro or anything like that. That would be silly. Yes, I have been lost. Yes, I feel contradictory things at the same time. Yes, I cannot feel that I know where my home is. No, I have not been in a civil war. It is just that his work suggests, makes hints. Also, there is this thing he does where he takes one item from normal life, a rake, a bird, and kind of paints one of them intensely, so it is like a bird with a capital B. I like that so much. I wish I could take one thing at a time and magnify it, so I can see every angle and line. Anything, everything. I want to do that with an idea, a picture, an ice-cream cone. Imagine being so focused that only one thing at a time existed. In my imagination, I would walk an ice cream all the way back to the farm, and the young girl doing her chores and milking the cow and coming in from the morning and being cold, and then the milk gets picked up and taken to a large, metal place, I imagine. Anyway, you get the picture; solitary and big, that is what Miro suggests, and that is another reason why I love him.

I wish there were a different type of apology I could give those I have hurt. With Joy and my aunt Debra, I think they want more than a general apology. They want specifics. But the specifics they want, I feel I don't have. They might want me to apologize in a very detailed way for the theft from the medicine cabinet. But I don't remember it, so I cannot. Joy would get angry with me for being imperious and impetuous—there was another "I" word in there that I cannot remember; was it *impulsive*? The thing is I don't want to do that, the apology, quite way they want it. I mean, do they want me to apologize for the way my brain works? You know what I mean?

My sponsor says it is good I don't live in regret. That I am not paralyzed. What I did is over. I am ready to move on. I am ready to like music and art again. There was this guy in rehab, Mark; I think that was his name. He was a pretty steady pot user, and, in fact, he never passed a drug test that they made us take. I was afraid he was going to have to get moved up to level 2, something that says your addiction is very serious. Yet I was a little baffled by him—it would never occur to me to just be a pothead. Pot makes everything like a fuzzy dream. Why settle there? I guess that goes back to liking Miro and that sense of blowing up.

Sometimes I think the drugs were a side trip to what is going to be a very unusual life anyway.

How can it not be? It already has been. These days, there is so much news about being bullied. My mom asks, "Oh, do you remember being bullied? The boy who threw your shoes out the window?" Of course, I remember. But what I want to say to her is that the bullying was not like what they say. The fear is terrible, and the victories are great. The victory of surviving. And the rewards I developed for myself—becoming lost in art, loving to climb very steep hills, bicycle rides at midnight. Somehow I thought drugs could be part of the reward system. Dumb idea.

What about those who did not survive the bullying? I know that is a very distinct possibility.

Some of the guys at rehab, when they talk about their past, it is very bothersome. I guess we drug users have fear and bullying in common. I am going to have to guess that was a common experience. Some of us took the tack that we should become bullies ourselves. Others were very fearful, seemed like they always were looking for a place to hide. I was spacey and lost in my own imagination. And we all ended up here at Intune Intensive Rehab Center. I think we would have ended up here anyway—bullying or not. But it would be a nice experiment, wouldn't it: If you were never bullied, would the drug use go down? Now, my sponsor would be mad at me for making anything that resembled an excuse, and I am not saying that if you are bullied you will use drugs. But I can imagine—I am allowed, aren't I? To imagine some big national grant that looked at us kids and bullies and drugs, and we would all go on Oprah and get to tell people that it just ain't a good thing, this bullying thing. And no one would listen to us, but for a moment, we could believe people cared about our experiences, our past, and want to help others and us.

That is the other thing. How am I going to grow up? That is one thing that I want. Even though I know sometimes that I remain a terrible child and see myself—my anger for not getting this or that.

During those times, I can be astonished at my meanness. I still want to be someone who does OK in the world. I do not know what Joan Miro's childhood was like, but I believe as a painter he must have been fascinated with his childhood and childhood in general. That he honored it. His paintings, they are childlike in how things are so impulsive and, I have to admit it, sort of unsmoothed. He is an adult who gets the whole weirdness of childhood.

Miro is always painting the night sky—well, not always but often. And in those paintings is a vastness so large it almost seems barren. And because of that, anything is possible in that night sky. My girlfriend and I were hiking, and it was funny: She loved being in the middle of the forest, surrounded by trees. I did not like that. My favorite part was being on top of the mountain, and there were no trees, for the most part. Or the trees were small because of a fire. That was what I liked, the smallness returning after destruction.

When my father got out of the psychiatric hospital, he lived in a halfway house. Supposedly, he was to tell them where he was going. But he said they never asked. He had a car, and why, I don't know. I guess he made a deal with some guy he lived with. If I know my father, he said he would cook for him or fill out forms in exchange for the use of the car. During those days, Frank would come to the house and just walk in. At first, my mom tried to be nice about it, but then she decided it would be best for everyone if she forbade him. Once, she stood in the driveway, and with her arms crossed, she said, "You may not come here like this; it is too hard on us." I remember thinking that I had never seen her like that. It was a kind of fierceness. I don't know. Theirs wasn't like typical divorces, where they split up the property and then spend the rest of their lives hating each other. Not like that at all. I always got the sense my mom was always hoping

Frank would snap out of it. We were not allowed to talk bad about him.

But one night, Joy and my sisters and I did have a laugh fest. It was Mia who brought up the topic: the weirdest thing our dad ever purchased for us from a thrift store. Joy talked about an

off-the-shoulder polka-dotted blouse. For Mia, it was boots with fringe. Tess couldn't think of anything. She said she wanted to close her eyes and keep them closed until his clothes for her were safely outside the house. She just did not want to know. I had a blazer once, it was sort of bright green, not quite a lime green but headed in that direction. Now, Frank had one like this, and he looked cool in it. He said you have to wear it with authority, and it would look good no matter what. He said you had to wear it with the secret knowledge that it was a good deal. Frank would say buying from a thrift store was one of the best ways to laugh at the bourgeois. It was a way of saying, "I don't need to buy from corporate hacks to look good." I liked the sentiment of that. Though I am not necessarily sure it was so true. We also remembered that once he came home with rubber sandals and matching belts—the sandals and belt matched, but also, and I wonder how he did this, there were sandals and belts for each of us. He imagined us as a family with matching rubber sandals and cheap belts.

After the crossing-the-arm thing that Joy did, he took to sneaking in my room during the middle of the night. He would use the side door of my room. I would leave it open for my girlfriend to sneak through, but Frank had also discovered that it was unlatched. Or sometimes he would knock on the window. It always startled me. And he would say, "I am just looking for a cigarette."

I would always ask, "How did you get here?"

He would tell me some convoluted story about how he traded cooking for one of the guys in exchange for the use of the car.

"Can you get in trouble for that?"

He would explain that no one cared and that "these half-way houses are a racket, another form of exploiting people for money. " He said he shared a small room with two other people. He had to walk sideways to get to his bed. That there was lots of bartering going on, like he did for the car. But he hated that people were exchanging drugs and no one cared. It spooked him. He talked about the difference between the mentally ill and drug users. He said that if you were crazy, you were unpredictable; if you were a drug user, the biggest problem was you were not trustworthy. So he was upset that they were all mixed up together. No one was going to get better with that mix, and no one cared. He was going to get out. He just needed to figure it out.

He told me once that he didn't miss Joy. I was afraid to ask him if he missed us kids. I was afraid of what he might say. Sometimes he would just look at me with this confused glance, "Why am I here?"-type thing. I appreciated his visits in a strange way. It made me feel like I was an anchor, and maybe he looked up to me for that.

"Hey, man," he once said, "I think you get it."

"Get what?" I asked.

"How amazing and hard it is to have these communications going on," he said.

I think I do get it. A little, I think. But I don't really want to have this in common with my father. I'd rather have other things in common with him. I like the way he made Joy happy with his cooking and the kind way he brought her secondhand shoes and blouses. It always surprised Joy—sometimes in a good way.

That was what I wanted, to not be afraid to be surprising to others or myself. I think I came close to that once. I painted my girlfriend, Rose, as a rocking librarian. She had these very conservative clothes on but was sort of doing the twist. I painted her from the neck down, so you would only know it was her by her small wrists and shoulders, and also it was on wood. I liked that, and I had no idea where the concept came from, but I went with it. I trusted it. Frank was able to trust himself, no matter how idiosyncratic he was. And I don't think that was because he was crazy. It was more like, at the end of the day, he knew what he was—or he knew his strengths. And knew how to describe his fears—like the fear of having a steady job—not as fears but as different things. Like beating the system, raising the kids, creating. Now, at the end of the day, we knew that was bullshit. But it worked for him, for us, his family, for a very long time. Problem was, when it quit working, it was a disaster.

I am not sure why it quit working. But the theory I have, and I learned it in rehab, is that you have to be scrupulously honest, or things will not work out. Maybe Joy and Frank never really took the time or were able to say, "There is a problem here." About Frank, you know. I don't know if they did. They were more than likely to call my father's thrift-store binge *a bad day* or *eccentric*. It was like it never occurred to them that there is a problem here with a grown man actually hiring a delivery truck to drop off broken furniture, bikes and ugly clothes to your house. Yes, Joy would get that squinty-eyed look and tighten her lips. Sometimes she would bring Frank to the doctor's. Too often, though, she would ask him what his intentions were for this stuff. Kind of like, "And how was your day?"

One thing I learned about Miro, because I chose him for a research topic in my art class, is that he tried to have a normal life. He went to business school, he tried to work, but then he had a nervous breakdown. This is what was said in this book my aunt Debra read to me. He had a nervous breakdown. Did I have a nervous breakdown? Was I worn out by trying to be something I was not? How can that be when I don't even know what I am? I just know what I am not. I am not a lifetime drug user, I am not going to be a banker, I am not going to be a team guy, I am not going to charm my way to anyone's top of anything. But other than that, I do not know.

Miro said he was completely and always astonished by the night sky. And he made it, in a way, his life's work. I can understand that. The night sky is one of my most favorite things. And to see the moon tilt and change colors. To wonder how the moon can change the sky. Miro looked to the night sky for inspiration because of its vastness. Yet there is nothing vast about his work; it is blown out, and it is big and consuming, not at all like the blankness of the sky that he says inspires him. Yet each painting hints at that vastness.

I am not trying to say everything is about me. That Joan Miro painted with someone like me in mind. But I can feel crowded and vast. How I wish that, now that I have found love in Rose, I could say I am done. It is complete, the facts of my life. I have tried that angle even as a kid, trying to be certain. I would find myself saying to myself that this satisfaction, this flavor of ice cream, would complete and end my longing. Later, this drug would make my life. But sometimes, when I look at Miro, I think the question is, "Can I be all right with the incompleteness?"

And I don't think I can. I am afraid of it. Even though I am not even sure I know what it is. That was why I was afraid to ask Frank if he missed us. If he said yes, then his life is unsatisfactory. If he said no, then it would mean he has moved on from us, that we no longer matter. As ill and weird as Frank is, I still want him to want us.

I wanted to investigate this notion of who I was to my father. So once when he came over at 2:00 a.m., I said I did not have cigarettes. I wanted to see if he would stay even if I had nothing to offer, no cigarettes. He looked devastated. I said, "Frank, you can still come to visit. It doesn't have to be really be about cigarettes, does it?" I don't know why I had never thought to say that before.

Then he started to tell me about how, when he was young, he and his friends decided to go to San Francisco and protest the election of Ronald Reagan as president. He said he got the idea of making a video of the demonstration. He said one of the challenges of making a video is that you have to walk backward. But it helped him understand history in a new way. He learned that going backward takes a toll on you; it is physically very hard. He became more convinced by walking backward with a camera that we cannot go back to the good old days, like Reagan wanted.

And I asked, "What about the present, Frank? That can be kind of hard on you too." I told him about Joan Miro. I am not sure what I said exactly, but I know I was emphatic.

I told my father how Miro had studied to be a business-type person, but he fell apart. He had a nervous breakdown. So he created a future for himself as an artist. Then surrealism happened and the Spanish Civil War, and it was hard, but he was determined to carve out a moment for himself in a small house in France. That was where he went because of the war. Miro would work and look at the sky. And what he imagined there, he would paint. Miro, to survive, could not think about the future or the past but only how to paint what he envisioned was in that sky. What about that, Frank?

Frank nodded his head slowly and said, "You really like this guy Miro? Jake, what would your night sky have in it?" Now this was a little astonishing because it meant Frank had stopped and listened to me. I was almost destroyed because I was so excited by this.

I said, "Some of the things Miro had—rakes, wheels, broken items." I realized then that by putting those things in my night sky, I was putting Frank in. "I would put you in, Frank, but not you, the things you love. I would make a corner of the sky filled with dishes, and they would symbolize you right after one of the great meals you have made. Let's say Thai food." That made us laugh, like we were imagining Thai food in a Spanish sky.

"I am really glad you would put me in, Jake. You would be in my night sky. All of you would be, even your mother; she would be a tiny star, a distant galaxy, but one that has gotten me here, smoking cigarettes with my only and, therefore, favorite son."

I am almost a grown man, but I started to cry. And I just said what I didn't know I wanted to say: "I miss you. I see your eyes, and I miss you. And I know that you will not be coming back this time like you were. I can see it in your eyes. They have left us. And I think back on the times you were there, as part of our family. Your crazy purchases and then being all frugal at the thrift store. I knew you, man, and I don't anymore."

"Yeah, I know, son, but remember it hurts to go backward. It hurts the back of your legs. It hurts you. But, man, you have made my life extraordinary, each of you." And then he brought up the time the kids in the bus took off my shoe and threw it out the window. Obviously, this made quite the mark on Frank and my mother; they both recently had brought it up. "That time on the bus. It would hurt to go back there, right? But you know why that kid got mad at you? Because you were singing. I think it was 'Hey Jude' or something. And he told you to stop, and you did not. You kept singing. And that is what I want for you more than anything, that you keep singing, man. Keep singing."

Then he started to cry. And that annoyed me, I have to admit, because I had to stop my crying and hold my dad. I said, "Thank you for everything," though I did not know what that was. But you know what? He wasn't listening. I could tell that. I was trying to thank my father, and he could not listen.

He said, "Son, maybe I will move back to my roots, the great Puget Sound, the Pacific Ocean."

And I said, "But I thought we just decided that the past hurt. Isn't that your past? Wouldn't that hurt?"

Frank stared at me and then out at the endless sky, and he smiled a little and shrugged his shoulders. "Yeah, that is true," he said. "But you have to admit it is a pretty good idea, don't you think?"

"Why?" I asked.

Frank said, "Well, you should see the water there. It is like your night sky. You could visit, Jake. I can only imagine what your imagination would make of the silky gray water of the Puget Sound."

God, how that pleased me. Frank was thinking of me as a part of his future. I was part of his imagination. Could a son ask for anything more?

Sister Joan Clara gets permission to take a painting class

I ran into Joy at the art museum today. It has been a while since she has been in to see me. We in the religious community do not take these things personally. We know God's door is revolving. I was happy to see her, and she seemed pleased too. She had fewer shadows around her eyes, and so I assumed she had gotten a job—that was the most important thing to her when she would visit.

I asked, "Good news about the job?"

"No," she said, "but the kids are doing well." I have seen these cases before—when Joy was with me, she must have misperceived her greatest worry. She must have thought she needed a job to help her kids to be OK. But she must have learned at some point they needed her to be OK. Clearly, she understood that—she was here at an art museum. Meaning she was OK or working on being OK. This is what made her kids "good," not her status as employed or not employed.

Still, I said, "I'll keep praying."

"Yes, please do," she returned. "What brings you here, Sister?" she asked.

I told her I am taking a watercolor class, and this exhibition is an assignment. It is a faculty show, and my teacher has two paintings on display. My teacher is large and expansive, in body and personality. He gave his advice in a large and booming voice. "Sister JC," he called me, "think texture, texture, texture."

I needed to get permission to take the class. I needed to explain how it would help the community and help God. You might think that was an easy task, but it was not. I thought about it quite a bit. I knew they would say yes, but I still knew it was important to take the question seriously. When I went to the committee to make my case, there were six nuns. They kept asking me to speak up. That was one of the more difficult requests they had. When you spend your life in contemplative prayer and speaking to God, loud and verbal can be very challenging.

Anyway, I told the sisters my story. I was the second-oldest of eight. The oldest girl. I did not want to be a nun, but Father was very religious and very intent on this pathway. I went to live with this order, the Benedictines, because I was pretty sure they would see I was not fit and would kick me out because I was nervous and fidgety. I didn't see how they could tolerate me in a contemplative environment. However, it turns out they only turn down those who have debt and those who have a mental illness. I then made a deal with God. I was a young woman at the age of nineteen. I wanted God to let me know if I was crazy. If I was crazy, clearly I would need to go. If I was not crazy, I would stick it out and stay in the convent. But I wanted to know soon if I was crazy so I could quit fighting my life. I woke up a week later to a chattering in my ears. "Voices," I thought, somewhat happily. "I must be crazy. I am going to get to leave the convent."

I spent a week in the hospital undergoing psychiatric exams and physical tests. It turns out I have tinnitus—it appears I had damage in my inner ear. I have struggled with it the whole thirty-five years I have been here. God won!

I have done many assignments. I have been the convent bookkeeper, the space manager, and I started the gift shop. This is what was needed. Now, I told the sisters, the community may not know they need this, and I don't know how it will reveal itself in practical ways, but the community needed me to answer the bright and beautiful colors I saw each morning when I prayed. It was time to manifest what I saw in my soul to a canvas. I knew that. I had prayed about it. I know I must begin to make real the colors. I know this as a matter of fact, like I know the days of the week.

It is so odd how we confuse our conversations with God. How we try to make God "ours" instead of something like water. That is what I told the sisters. I didn't know if I was going to paint a masterpiece or even something pleasant we could hang. I just knew I was going to have my next level of conversation with God. I said I wanted to release the color on the inside of me. I also spoke of Hildegard de Bergenvon Bingen, how in the Middle Ages she was noted for being a successful convent administrator. Today, she is known as a poet and musician. I did not compare myself to her but only wanted to say the present is a mystery, and so is the future, but they are both equally real. We cannot ask ourselves what the meaning of things is, only what is genuine at this moment. Painting was the answer I had received.

I have considered leaving the convent many times, and my decisions to stay have not always been spiritual. I have made the decision on occasion because I am comfortable here and secure. I love the prayer and singing. The kindest thing God has done is to fill me with color; this has happened over the past two years. It seems to be a dark color—a tree going up in a jagged sort of way to a hole in the heavens. The inner edges of the hole are an amazing orange, and the sky behind the hole is an astonishing blue. I may never get the blue right, but I want to try. The committee said yes. That means I can say yes too.

Frank takes refuge

I am very pleased with myself. That I was able to get, for my own possession, this van. I thought I negotiated very well. I did have to strike a deal with Joy for a little cash, but I also cooked for three months for a family from Yemen to get this.

I met Maraud, a refugee from Yemen, the father of two beautiful girls and a diligent, dutiful husband, when I was walking in the early morning. I am not sure how I struck up a conversation with him. I think I just simply observed, "Nice van." He was working under the hood of a blue Chevy van.

He replied with a smile, "Do you want to buy it?"

I hadn't thought about that at all, but I said, "Sure."

Then the whole plan came to me and made sense. Buy this blue Chevy van, pack up and go back to where I began. I had been thinking for quite some time that it might be good for me, for us, Joy and the kids, if I went back home to Washington State. I grew up there. And I just wanted that landscape again. The water and even the grayness. I wanted to be able to walk and pick fruit you can actually eat. I wanted the ethnic groceries and interesting spices. The thought was refuge, not escape. I am prepared to rebuild.

I met Maraud in March, nearly two years after all of the

shit hit the fan for my family and me. Since then, things have gotten better for me and even Joy. She has gotten a job. Not a great one, as I understand it. But she is diligent, and things could get better for her, I am sure. If that is what she wants. If what she desires is money and authority in her job, she could have that, I am sure. It is just hard to tell. I don't think I know her anymore. I used to be able to help her when she would work late hours in hopes of doing well on a project. It is like she still wants to do a good job because that is her habit, but it is not for any real ambition. It is not to make sure the kids get super-great whatever—tutors, camps and vacations.

Jake is doing well. Sober nearly for two years. I have been stable for nearly as long, maybe fourteen months. After the hospital, they moved me into a halfway house. Then I was able to get a small apartment. So I have my own type of sobriety behind me, I guess. No erratic behavior, and that is why I could pull this move off to Washington State. It was quite the process. So many people had to approve, especially my caseworker. And I had to talk my girlfriend into coming. I am not sure what I would have done if she had said no.

The small apartment I shared with my girlfriend was on the far east side of town, very far from Joy and the children, but it had sidewalks. It might have been the sidewalks that got me thinking about my hometown in the Northwest. I realized that in the neighborhoods where Joy and I and the children had lived, there had been no sidewalks, no solid foundation to place your foot as you walked. I really enjoyed the sidewalk, and it reminded me of the small town where I had grown up. There were rows of World War II bungalows lined along cement walkways up and down each street.

I cooked for Maraud and his family for three months.

That was the deal: I would do cooking, help with English and come up with $2,500. In exchange, he would have a solid, running car for me. I don't think his wife was able to cook. I think she was depressed. She seemed to sit in an armchair and watch television, pretty much expressionless. I assumed for the full day she sat there, but I don't really know for sure. I was supposed to get the family used to American cooking. "American cooking is not my thing," I told Maraud. He shrugged his shoulders as if to say, "Is it anybody's thing?"

I did help out with the English, a little. I thought we could use some poems I had written for my lessons with the girls. I think my reasoning was sound—that I would be a better teacher if we were working on something I could be very enthusiastic about. But Maraud had a good point too. He just wanted his two daughters, third- and fifth-graders, to do well in school and pass any required test so he would not be harassed. I understood, very completely. After my public breakdown and the trouble and pain it caused, I had a very deep appreciation of understanding what it would be like to be under the radar. I used to want to be noticed, but now I want the quiet. A few solid moments of quiet each morning, and then I am ready.

I went into the small, crammed kitchen and did homework with the kids. They were cute and diligent and asked me questions about where popsicles come from. At first, none of them, Maraud and his children, believed I had children. So I had to dig up a photograph and bring it to them.

Those children, Aisha and Dayeah, were quite delightful. We never got very close; we stayed formal, but our relationship was easy. I think all of us were very goal-oriented. I told the older one, Aisha, about the five-paragraph rule and how you can expand each paragraph by asking yourself "why" three times: Why did the friends have an argument? Why did they make up? Why did they make up at home and not at school? She seemed to like that but started confusing why and how. When I asked how did they get to the United States, instead of saying an airplane, she said, "Because my family needs money, and my father is afraid of the military." It made for interesting conversations.

Her younger sister, Dayeah, was a little more playful. She was a third-grader and studying comparisons. I couldn't tell if she was playing with me when she compared a stapler to a television. I asked her how so? She observed that staplers keep things together like papers, and televisions keep families together. I must have looked puzzled. Then she pointed at her mother in front of the television set. "That television is keeping my mom out of my father's way. That is a good thing," she whispered.

After an hour or so with the children, I would begin the meal. I had negotiated no cleaning of the dishes, and so, after cooking, I just went home, strolled the one mile to my small apartment. They liked my cooking. They never complained. I think they liked my macaroni and cheese the best that I doctored with hot sauce and pimiento olives.

I wanted Joy's blessing for this move. I wanted her to like this, even though I am not sure it would have mattered, I am so determined. I guess we had been through so much together. So I asked her to meet me at the park without the children. I could tell that made her nervous. She had not been alone with me. I don't think she was afraid of me. Maybe she made a promise to someone that she would not be alone. Maybe it was herself she didn't trust. It was like she was brimming over with some unknown emotions, and she had decided it was not useful to investigate much of anything with me, only what involved the children. She was kind, but no part of her belonged to me. And it was the same for me. I no longer felt her under my skin, in my psyche. Is this the way the war-wounded feel? A constant vague and fearful anticipation, especially around those things that have been the source of terror.

Joy did meet me, on her way to work; she must have wanted a built-in time limit. She looked a little startled when I told her I wanted to move back to Washington State. I knew children would be her biggest concern. Over the months, we had developed our own routines. The five of us would get together at a city park near their home. At first, we tried to do the whole cookout thing. But that was too elaborate. So we would have fruit and water; sometimes we all showed up empty-handed. I think we, Joy and I, were proud of that. We could be together as a family and be empty-handed. There was a simple truth about that.

Joy was stern at first, talking about her concerns for the children. I had prepared well for this situation. I said it would be a great place for all of them to visit. I could see that resonate with Joy. She still had her good friend Roxanne there, and she often thought it was unfortunate that we didn't know my family well. She wanted guarantees that I would not lose contact and reminded me of how terrible it would be if we lost contact.

"Joy," I said, "in the worst of times, I never lost contact." I tried to make a joke and remind her of the times I had too much contact. She put her hand up to signal "stop," but she smiled—maybe thinking back to that distant place of our madness? She agreed, almost easily. Maybe it was because Joy had her own memories of the Northwest, with its lushness and abundance. And she said she thought with me being there, the kids could have access to it, though the kids were growing up and would be creating their own memories soon. I hoped Joy understood that.

When I mentioned my girlfriend was coming with me, Joy gave a very sad nod. I didn't want to think about that, the nod. What it might mean, that nod. She can be so inscrutable, that Joy. I was going to pick my girlfriend, Linda, up in Los Angeles, where she was visiting her sister. Maybe Joy was sort of happy, to tell the truth. Maybe it gave her comfort to know I would not be navigating alone. Maybe she also thought she could get on with her own life now.

The truth is my relationship with the children and Joy has been stripped down to the bone. For them and for me. I think at one time Joy would have wanted me to either make money or be a better stay-at-home parent, and it was so painful to not be those things for her. But knowing my limitations has been necessary to save my life—that and to say them out loud to myself and others, not with anger like I used to but like I was reading the newspaper. A simple story on the back page: "Man has limits. Grocery shopping, walking, going to the doctor's, a movie is the right amount of things for a day and a lifetime."

Joy did give me money for the car. I hated to take it. I know times have not been good to her. But I had to play hardball with her. I was that sure that getting to the Northwest was the right thing to do, and that was what fortified me as I reminded her of the days in the hospital basement, the misery I have been in. Then, in a very calm way, I also reminded her that, officially, because I stayed at home with the children, she still owed me some money, alimony. I hated myself a little for reminding her of that.

She had no money, and I didn't want to bring up any of our history, but I have this deal with myself: try to do what is necessary, even if it is hard. And that was what I felt about leaving this town and returning to the Northwest. Joy looked pained when I said this. But, then, Joy always looks pained.

I don't know how she came up with the money, though I kind of bet her sister and her friend Angela gave it to her. I am sure they were happy to see me go. They may think it was a good deal, $2,500 to get me out of town. I don't blame them. On certain days, I can understand what it looked like to them. Someone incapable of being with the amazing Joy. But it wasn't like that always.

Joy and I had a great deal of fun and caring. It was the secrets that did us in. Maybe she had her own. I had mine. That I was scared mostly. That I did not know how to negotiate her needs, her middle-classness, and my very own roots. I am so happy I don't have to do that dance ever again. It nearly destroyed me and Joy and the children.

I like the routines Linda and I have. A day for people like us, those who have doctors to see, can be full. Just the transportation of getting to where we need to go. It is nice to have one person on your team. Joy tried, but she was so distracted. I do admire all that she has on her plate and that she faces it each day. But I do not feel sorry for her like her sister does or her friend Angela. She made her life. She could have understood her own anguish better and her own conflicting desires—me and normalcy—but she didn't.

God, I am going to miss my kids, Jake with his love of my

history; Tess, the one I knew the best, the one that was mine more than Joy's; and Mia, such a smart kid.

Something was different about this move for me. I was not being impulsive but enthusiastic. Almost mindful. Sometimes you just have to sit down and be quiet with yourself. And the thing about that is the whole suffering becomes clear. Not just that I have suffered, but we all have. All of us humans, of course. But Joy and the children, right now and especially. When suffering has become so paramount you just need to seek refuge, a place of comfort. Though I am a grown man with children of my own, I wanted to go where I was with my mother, who has been dead since shortly after Tess was born.

I wanted to go and be near water. Vast water—my roots. I am just a middle-aged man, but I feel so old, and an old man needs to return to where he began. It is not like me to be this literal, and that is why I trust this move. No more symbolism for me, just the ground beneath my feet, my very own ancient ground. And Linda with her beautiful skin, and her own history and her own desire for peace.

Joy and I told the kids together during one of our park visits. Then Joy wanted me to take each kid separately "so they could each have something in their psychological pocket," I think was the way Joy described it. She loves the symbolic, what can be taken away. And she said to all of us in forced cheerfulness, "Just see it as another reorganization of the family." We all started throwing things at her, paper plates, cups, in a playful way, because we all had been through her reorganizations before. She smiled a little.

Jake first, of course. He looked at me with these steely

blue eyes. And then he just started to cry. He just said it, the thing we were all afraid of. "What if I never see you again? What if you die? Here I see you, even if it is infrequent and kind of supervised by her," meaning Joy, of course. "Now, with you gone, I will have to imagine you all the time." I told him how I couldn't wait for him to visit, that where I grew up you could walk along the coast and look for crabs, and we would do that. I said that we might be in touch even more because we knew how difficult it would be to be separated and also difficult to call up and get together.

Tess, oh, Tess. Tess gave me something, a holy card she had. It was a picture of Saint Anthony, the patron saint of lost things, she told me. I wanted her to know that she was not lost; she never would be. I knew exactly where I was going to post this card, I told Tess. I was going to tape it on the dashboard of my car so I could look at it as I was driving. I told her how I thought it was good to have saints looking after you, and I was happy to have Saint Anthony on my side. I told Tess she was a special girl, full of knowing how lost we could be, and that was good knowledge but could be scary because you could get lost in being so lost.

I don't know if Joy would have approved, but I told Tess that one of the most important things I have learned is to know that you are lost because only then can you ask for directions. I said we had been lost as a family. She agreed. I asked her how hurt had she been about everything? What did she think she had lost? "Oh, everything," she replied. "My father, and it will never be all right with my mom. I still can't figure a way to get along with her."

I hadn't seen before how angry Tess was, and I was surprised that it pissed me off somewhat. "Ah, Tess, why be the glass-half-empty sort of girl? Look how strong you have been and accomplished."

"I want an easier life," she said.

I told her how, when I was young, nineteen or so, I spent a summer on a fishing boat, and how you had to learn to walk kind of bowlegged as a way to keep your balance because the boat was always moving. And once this guy was just sick of doing it, and so he sat down on the boat near the ropes and just sat, so we needed to walk around him. He did this for three whole days, and finally we docked, and the captain fired him. I am not sure why I told her the story. I didn't want to have some neat little moral like "stay on the boat" or "walk any way you can, any way that keeps you afloat." I don't know why I told her the story, and when she looked at me blankly, I had nothing to offer, so I started to laugh. I made her promise to never take up smoking cigarettes and to teach me how to use Skype so we could talk often. Shit. I am going to need a computer, aren't I?

Mia surprised me. I wanted to tell her that she really kept me alive the way she would skip up the driveway after the bus would drop her off from school. That her skipping is still something I carry with me. But she didn't want any of that. She wanted advice on how to be frugal. She wanted to save money, and she thought her mom could use the help. Her mother's new job was nothing like the old one in its pay. "Well, I find that it is good to commit yourself to one thrift store and get to know it really well," I told her.

I advised her to not be disappointed if she could not find the most perfect thing right away. Just keep looking. The other thing was you needed to learn when the thrift store got its new shipments in, and that way if you timed your visit on that day, you would have the best chance of finding the best things. Mia shook her head and was even taking notes. That delighted me, I must say. She was worried that thrift stores had no-return policies. I told her I had a couple different opinions on that. The prevailing one is that it didn't matter that much because you were getting such a good deal anyway. The other opinion is that you could simply donate it to another thrift store and give someone else a chance.

Mia then told me that she wanted to write a novel on the painting "The Young Shepherdess." I didn't know it right away. So Mia described it as a girl in the 1800s looking out at us with this blue and silky background and the sheep barely visible. The painter had a fancy name, William-Adolphe Bouguereau. She said she wanted to imagine that girl's life away from being a shepherdess. I told her that was a good idea, a really good idea. And I asked her what she thought that life was like. "Well, no electricity," Mia said. "But with brothers, annoying brothers, and lots of duties. I am sure her duty did not end with the sheep. But I bet she was able to dream. If you look at her face, you know that she was able to dream."

I suppose I should have had one of those outings with Joy. I could have told her I love her and always will. I think she would have said the same thing to me. I almost asked for a private conversation with her, in person. Not one on the phone or in the park. But I couldn't bring myself to ask. What language could I use, what fractured and lyrical words could I string together to say, "What a life we made. So beautiful and damaged"?

Instead, I wrote her a letter. I wanted to say so many

things, but instead I found myself wondering to her about the Ten Commandments. How they might be a good way to live: not to steal, lie, hurt others. That somehow they had become passé, and I didn't want to be a born-again preacher, but they were a good idea. But so hard. How difficult it is to answer the question "How are you?" with any clarity. That it is a worthy ambition, isn't it, clarity and simple honesty? I had to be careful with this; "religious ideation" can be a bad sign for someone like me. But I didn't mean it that way, in an unrealistic or fanatical way. I wanted her to know that each day I was planning to be empty, so I would no longer be frightened. I don't know if she got it. I can imagine any claim of emptiness would probably upset her.

Hadn't I made her full, full with complications and despair? And trusted all of us could empty ourselves of that?

On my last day with Maraud's family, I made macaroni and cheese, with enough left over for a few weeks. Maraud and I shook hands and hugged. The girls and I shook hands. His wife got out of the chair, even. The room was dark. The room was always dark, so they were already silhouettes for me when I left them on the last night. But still I tried to plant them firmly in my heart so I would never forget them, my avenue home. That was how I always wanted to remember them.

I was planning on taking the scenic route after I picked up Linda. The sky-blue Chevy van was pretty well packed up. I had made a bed of pillows and a sleeping bag so we could avoid paying for hotel rooms. I had every love letter Joy had written next to me and notes from the kids. They had made a CD of their voices and their favorite songs, so I could listen on the road and have them with me. This was how Mia presented it. It was a strange compilation, screamo music from Jake, hip-hop from Tess and sort of folk from Mia.

On the morning I left, when I drove by to say the final goodbye, I watched and felt as Joy placed my face between her two hands. She stared so hard and squeezed me. Then she kissed me on the lips. That was when the crying began for all of us. Then I got in the car and drove away. It was that simple and that hard.

Joy

Frank went to Washington State, and I went to the grocery store. I was trying to be a decent and efficient cook. My new job, securing reference citations for a publishing company, was low pay, but I loved working. I loved knowing I was taking care of my children.

The same day Frank left, I clutched the grocery list. Clutched because it was the list that would sustain my family for one week. I did not want to lose it. While returning the grocery cart to its proper place, I saw Ted, my favorite homeless person. I shouted his name to him and reminded him that we had encountered each other before. I know I startled him, but he seemed significant to me. I asked him how he was doing.

He proceeded to tell me the most amazing story. That he had been clean nearly three months. If he could stay clean for two more weeks, he explained, he could move into the homeless shelter and even get trained for work.

He continued his story. How he had been using lots of street drugs. Any drugs he could find. At one point, he lost his girlfriend. He searched and searched for her but couldn't find her. He still has not found her.

After looking for a couple of days, he found some stairs

that were part of the town library. He stayed underneath the stairs because he was cool there, and there was a leaky sprinkler where he could get water. He couldn't find drugs, and he started to detox. He was too weak to leave, so he lived under the stairs, withdrawing and living off water and over-ripe fruit he found in garbage cans.

When he was strong enough to walk just a little, he found the soup kitchen. He said the remarkable thing was, when he started walking, he was thinking about food and not drugs. He wondered how he might get food, coffee, and, the strangest thing of all, he wanted new clothes. He knew there were certain parks he needed to stay away from because that was where his friends and drugs would be.

Someone from the soup line knew of safe places where he could stay, a library that was open twenty-four hours and a record store. Ted said he spends his days at the soup kitchen and is getting better. His girlfriend is lost, he sup-poses, a casualty of his, their, drug use.

I gave him twenty dollars and thanked him for his story. He smiled, did a little bow. I noticed he was walking with a limp. Probably from some old wound, I thought. I shouted at him, probably startling him again, "You'll be fine." He waved graciously, politely.

About the Author

*J*oy *Falls* is Barbara Allen's first novel. If she were given money for all the times this novel was a runner-up, she would be rich. She received an MFA from the University of Arizona in poetry. Her poetry has been published in literary journals, *Ploughshares, New England Review, Seattle Review,* and *Fine Madness*. She has received an Arizona Commission of the Arts fellowship and lives in Tucson, Arizona.

Made in the USA
Las Vegas, NV
09 February 2023

67179561R10148